"Where are you staying?" Nate asked.

Michelle frowned. "What do you mean? This is my home. I'm staying here."

"I have a contract that says you're not."

"You can't throw me out of my own house." Dread tightened like a fist in her gut.

"This badge says I can."

"Before we continue this argument, can you go feed your cat? The distressed cries are driving me crazy."

"What are you talking about? I don't have a cat."

She blinked in surprise. "Don't you hear that? It's been crying for the last five minutes."

He cocked his head as he listened. The plaintive wail came again, weaker now.

"That's not a cat." He moved to the front door, flung it open and charged coatless into the blizzard. "It's a—"

The wind grabbed his last word and garbled it, but it sounded as if he'd said *baby*.

Dear Reader,

Every little girl dreams of being a princess. Fairy tales foster the fantasies of life—peril, humor, love and happily-ever-after. It's my joy to bring you three stories based loosely on three fairy tales. This is Sleeping Beauty's story.

This book is dedicated to my nieces, and I'll share a story about Ashley. When she was in high school, she and three of her friends decided to dress up as princesses for Halloween, she chose Cinderella, and her mother helped her find a pretty blue dress that was full and swished when she moved. She put her blond hair up in a bun and wore long white gloves. She looked as if she'd walked from the pages of the fairy tale.

Sadly, she arrived on Halloween to find not one of her friends dressed up as promised. It could have been a disaster. Instead Cinderella became the belle of the ball. Everyone made a big deal of her all day long. And that evening, when she went trick-or-treating with her younger sisters, people praised her and asked if they could take her picture. That day she was a true princess.

Do you have a princess moment? I hope so.

Happy reading!

Teresa Carpenter

TERESA CARPENTER

The Sheriff's Doorstep Baby

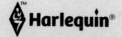

TORONTO NEW YORK LONDON
AMSTERDAM PARIS SYDNEY HAMBURG
STOCKHOLM ATHENS TOKYO MILAN MADRID
PRAGUE WARSAW BUDAPEST AUCKLAND

Recycling programs
for this product may
not exist in your area.

ISBN-13: 978-0-373-74181-6

THE SHERIFF'S DOORSTEP BABY

First North American Publication 2012

Copyright © 2012 by Teresa Carpenter

Teresa Carpenter believes in the power of unconditional love, and that there's no better place to find it than between the pages of a romance novel. Reading is a passion for Teresa—a passion that led to a calling. She began writing more than twenty years ago, and marks the sale of her first book as one of her happiest memories. Teresa gives back to her craft by volunteering her time to Romance Writers of America on a local and national level.

A fifth-generation Californian, she lives in San Diego, within miles of her extensive family, and knows that with their help she can accomplish anything. She takes particular joy and pride in her nieces and nephews, who are all bright, fit, shining stars of the future. If she's not at a family event, you'll usually find her at home—reading, writing or playing with her adopted Chihuahua, Jefe.

"Teresa Carpenter's *Her Baby, His Proposal* makes an oft-used premise work brilliantly through skilled plotting, deft characterization and just the right amount of humor."
—*RT Book Reviews*

Books by Teresa Carpenter

THE PLAYBOY'S GIFT
SHERIFF NEEDS A NANNY
THE BOSS'S SURPRISE SON

Other titles by this author available in ebook format.

For my nieces, Amanda, Ashley, Sammy,
Erika, Michelle, Gabrielle and Rachel.
You are everything a heroine should be:
beautiful, smart, talented and loving.
I'm proud of you all.

PROLOGUE

"DADDY! Daddy! You're here."

"Mama! Hi! Over here."

Arms flung wide, ten-year-old Michelle Ross twirled in a wide circle, her long blond curls and wide pink skirt flowing out around her. She determinedly ignored the excited calls of her friends as their parents arrived to visit.

For the first time ever she felt beautiful.

She loved Princess Camp, even if her dad didn't come to parents' day. He said he would, but he promised lots of things that didn't happen. Duty first.

She begged and begged Daddy to be able to come. And of course, he said no. And continued to say no until Aunt Yvonne finally stepped in to plead Michelle's case. She had to behave all of June and July—which had been torture—but come August she'd been off to camp. And all that boring good behavior paid off.

She shared a cabin with Elle and Amanda. They instantly became BFFs and did everything together. And Michelle loved it all, even the etiquette classes. A princess needed to know how to conduct herself!

"Michelle, these are my parents." Dragging a dark-haired man by his hand, Elle proudly presented her father. "Daddy, Mama, Michelle is in my cabin. She's Beauty. I'm Belle and Amanda is Rapunzel. We're going to do a dance for the talent show. Sleeping Beauty had the gift of song, so Michelle's going to sing."

"Hello, Michelle." Elle's father greeted her and shook her hand. "What a lovely young woman you are. I can see why you're Beauty."

She giggled and dropped into a shallow curtsy. "It's so nice to meet you."

"What lovely manners," Elle's mother said with a kind smile.

"The pleasure is all ours." Her dad tugged on Elle's dark red ponytail. "I can't wait to see you girls dance. And to hear you sing, Michelle."

"The talent show isn't until after dinner,"

Elle advised him. "Come on. I want to show you my cabin, and the pool, and the gazebo."

He laughed indulgently. "We're coming, Elle. But what about your friend?"

"Oh. Michelle's waiting for her dad. Right?"

"Yes—" Michelle nodded and put hope into her voice "—he should be along anytime."

Elle's mom looked down the empty drive and frowned. "I don't like leaving you alone out here."

"I have to stay in the courtyard," Michelle reassured her. "I'll be fine."

"Elle, I think we should ask your friend to keep us company until her dad comes along."

"Yeah." Elle grabbed Michelle's hand, swung it back and forth. "Come with us. Your dad can find us when he gets here."

"Maybe." Michelle bit her lip. She should wait for Daddy. She was excited to show her dad around camp, to tell him what she'd learned, and how much she loved her time here. More than anything she wanted him to hear her sing and to impress on him that she should come back next year. But the truth was he probably wouldn't even show. He meant his promises when he made them, yet the need to protect and serve took first place every time.

But Elle's daddy thought Michelle was pretty and she wanted to go with them.

"I guess I can look around with you until he gets here."

"Yippee!" Elle smiled and together they skipped ahead.

They showed Elle's parents the cabin and the pool. And when they headed back to the main cabin, The Castle, Michelle looked around hopefully and glanced toward the parking lot, but saw no sign of her dad.

She got ready for the talent show with Elle and Amanda and pretended not to be nervous as she checked the audience repeatedly for her father.

"Come on, Michelle." Amanda grabbed her hand and tugged her away from the wings. "It's our turn."

Michelle frantically searched the crowd one last time but there was no denying the inevitable. Another promise broken. Daddy wouldn't see her sing. She sighed her disappointment and followed her friends onstage.

CHAPTER ONE

HANDS braced on his hips, Sheriff Nate Connor stood looking down at the strange beauty sleeping on his couch. Rolled up in his fleece throw, purple-and-pink-striped socks peeked out from one end and sunshine-yellow hair cascaded from the other.

With a muffled curse he holstered the nine millimeter he'd palmed when he found his front door unlocked. Not that he'd really expected to need it, but a soldier was always prepared. Even in River Run, where the population was less than five thousand.

Luck and skill had kept him from shooting himself when he tripped over the guitar case negligently left in the entry hall.

He considered reaching for his handcuffs, but the woman wasn't a complete stranger. He'd seen sufficient pictures here in this house and on his predecessor's desk to recognize the pretty flow of hair. He was enough of a lawman to figure out she was his new landlord.

And they'd met briefly at her father's funeral seven months ago.

Yeah, he knew who sleeping beauty was. The question was why?

Why was she here and why did she think she could make herself at home on his couch?

He'd had his own plans for that couch. Today was supposed to have been his first day off in over a month. The storm changed that. An overnight delivery truck had skidded on ice and ended up on its side in the pass, blocking traffic in both directions. By the time they got it cleared up, they were in the middle of a full-blown blizzard, and he'd given up any hope of regaining his day off.

A surge of wind knocking branches against the house punctuated the thought.

After a ten-hour day, he'd planned to come home, heat up a frozen dinner and watch the game he'd recorded earlier.

Plans delayed by his uninvited guest's possession of said couch.

A soft snore came from the fleece-wrapped bundle. Nate's dark brows slammed together in a scowl. Now that was irritating. Not because the sound annoyed him, but because it didn't. It had been cute.

He had no room in his life for soft and cute, no patience for trespassing blondes interrupting the last of his day off.

In the past seven months he'd heard nothing from Michelle Ross. Now she slept tucked up on his couch. She may own the place but he had a contract stating it was his for the next four months. He didn't know what brought her to town, but she wasn't staying here.

A matter he meant to take up with her right now.

"Ms. Ross."

No response.

"Ms. Ross." Advancing on the couch, he repeated the demand for her attention, and then again, louder each time. She stirred and then settled against the cushions, sighing as she pulled the throw tighter around herself.

Finally he leaned down and shook her shoulder. "Come on, beauty, wake up."

She stirred and mumbled something.

Instinctively, he leaned closer to hear what she said.

But suddenly she turned and her lips brushed

his. That's when her eyes opened. Lovely eyes that brought the green of spring to a late-winter's storm. And that thought distracted him long enough for her to wrap her arms around his neck and draw him down for a deeper kiss.

Questions of who and why and what disappeared in a rush of sensation. She felt warm and soft, and tasted oh, so sweet. This was what home should feel like, what a welcome should taste like.

Nate threaded his hands in all that hair and sank into the moment. After the day he'd had, he let the heat of the kiss sweep him away.

Michelle dreamed of a man on a white horse riding through the forest. Tall and strong, he carried a sword and sought a beautiful princess, ready to save her from all her woes. Michelle was both the princess and not. She liked the safety the knight represented, but it never came free and she wanted to save herself.

Only fools and optimists believed in love. Which left her out. She was nobody's fool. And she'd given up on optimism early in life. She preferred to control her own destiny than hope for the best.

Now the knight was on top of her, holding

her gently, his hands fisted in her hair, broad shoulders blocking out the world. He smelled like the fleece that held her in warmth and comfort, of the woods and man. But he was heat and power and his lips were on hers and she didn't care if there was a price. Safe had never felt so good.

She arched into the kiss, opening her lips at the demand of his, welcoming him in, savoring the spicy taste of the man who held her so securely.

His hand moved in a sweeping caress from her head to her waist, where skin met skin. The shock of his cold fingers reached beyond Michelle's lethargy.

Her eyes flew open and she realized this was no dream, no Prince Charming of childish imaginings, but a flesh-and-blood man with a bold kiss and cold hands.

She broke off the kiss, planted both palms flat against his chest and pushed. "Back up, buddy!"

For a moment, just a heartbeat, he held the embrace, and then he released her and surged to his feet.

"Hell. I must be more tired than I thought." He scrubbed both hands over a face a shade too ordinary to be considered handsome. Straight dark eyebrows topped fierce gray eyes. Cut military-short, his hair was a tawny blend of brown, blond and red. Temper, or maybe it was passion, brought a ruddy hue to his cheeks.

The khaki uniform so like her father's had her narrowing her eyes on him as she swung her feet to the floor and sat up. Pain throbbed in her ankle, but she ignored it.

"Who are you and what are you doing in my house?" she demanded. "Besides accosting me?"

"You mean my home?" His hands went to his hips, and he met her glare for glare. "And you kissed me."

She raised brows at him. "A neat trick for someone asleep. I inherited this house from my father."

"And I rented it from him."

That surprised her. "He didn't tell me anything about renting the house. When did that happen?"

"Ben rented me a room when I first moved to town and I continued to rent the place when he moved in with his lady friend almost a year ago."

"Dad had a girlfriend?" She'd been dreaming of princesses and white knights, but clearly she'd fallen down the rabbit hole. As far as she knew, Dad had never had a lady friend.

"I remember you now, from my father's funeral." Usually great with names, she reached for his and came up short. The funeral had been hard for her. She took a stab. "Gabe?"

"Nate." He corrected. "Nate Connor."

"Well, Nate, it seems you took over Dad's job, and you took over his house."

His expression frosted over. "What are you implying?"

"Nothing nefarious." She waved off his paranoia. "I'm just saying this is my house."

She'd only come back to River Run to sell the house so she could move to Los Angeles and pursue her songwriting career.

She'd escaped this town when she graduated from high school—couldn't leave the little burg fast enough—and nothing had changed since. With her dad's passing the small town had even less going for it now than it had when she was a kid.

So no, she hadn't crept through Dead Man's

Pass praying to a deity she hadn't spoken to in way too long to be kicked out of her own home.

"It's your house, but it's rented to me. I have a contract if you'd like to see it." Nate crossed his arms over his chest, causing his biceps to pop. "You didn't talk to your dad much, did you?"

The truth she'd come to acknowledge since her dad's passing hit her hard. Hearing the censure from the current sheriff didn't help.

"You don't know anything about my relationship with my father." Anger had her pushing to her feet. The ankle she'd injured walking up the snow-covered path from the car to the front door protested at the sudden motion, at the sudden weight, and gave out on her.

He caught her before she could fall, putting those impressive biceps to work, his grip under her elbows easily holding her weight off the sore foot.

"Are you okay?" Exasperation sat alongside concern in the question.

"Fine." She attempted to shrug off his touch, but he held firm until she was seated once again. "I tripped on something on the way up the walk."

He frowned. "I'll check it out tomorrow. Do you need ice for your ankle?"

It irked to hear him playing host in her house. She shook her head. "I'm fine. How long did you know my dad?"

"Three years," he said as he shrugged out of his jacket and hung it on the newel post.

She waited, hearing the cry of a kitten in the lull, but that was all he shared. Great. Her father had been the same all her life, bound by duty, determined to steal all the joy from her life. Now it seemed there'd been more to him than she remembered, but the bearer of the news was no more talkative than her father had been.

"Not very long," she challenged.

"Not compared to twenty-five years, no. But I talked to him, worked with him, spent time with him. You let a complete stranger make funeral arrangements."

Shame burned in her. That had been the lowest time in her life. A bad week capped off by the loss of her father. Yeah, she should have come home and taken care of the details of Dad's funeral, but she'd been trying to save her job, trying to hold together the fraying edges of her life.

In the end she'd only been delaying the inevitable.

"I thanked you for your help." She tried to find a smile and a little of her patented charm to ease the way with him. She'd learned early in life that a pretty girl had power, and she wielded the tool of her looks like any other talent.

But she was too weary, too annoyed with him and the crying of his cat, to bother. Or maybe she was too unsettled by the taste of him still in her mouth to summon a smile.

And what had that been about anyway? She was supposed to have kissed him in her sleep? Right.

So okay, she'd been kissing the knight in her dream. Coincidence. By no means did that translate into smooching a stranger in her sleep.

"Huh." He dismissed her claim of gratitude. "Where are you staying?"

She frowned. "What do you mean? This is my home, I'm staying here."

"I have a contract that says you're not."

"You can't throw me out of my own house."

Dread tightened like a fist in her gut. She couldn't afford to pay for alternative accommodations.

"This badge says I can."

"Please." She gestured to her swollen foot. "I couldn't leave if I wanted. I can't drive."

He drew a set of keys from his pants pocket. "I can take you wherever you need to go."

Sleet blew against the window as the wind roared, a timely reminder of the harsh weather.

"I'm not leaving." Defiant, she crossed her arms over her chest and made a show of settling back into the couch. The tension from the long trip was back as she faced being expelled from her own home, the stress aggravated by the cries of distress from the kitten deep in the house.

"Oh, you are."

She shook her head, holding up a staying hand. "Before we continue this argument, can you go feed your cat? The distressful cries are driving me crazy."

"What are you talking about? I don't have a cat."

She blinked in surprise. "Well, then one is

trying to get in. Don't you hear that? It's been crying for the last five minutes."

This should be interesting. Would the big bad sheriff help the stray or leave it to fend for itself in the storm he was so ready to toss her out into?

He cocked his head as he listened. The roaring wind covered the sound for a moment and then the plaintive wail came again, weaker now. Poor kitty.

"That's not a cat." Suddenly his expression changed, became harder—something she couldn't have imagined—and determined. Urgent now he moved to the front door, flung it open, and charged coatless into the blizzard. "It's a—"

The wind grabbed his last word and garbled it, but it sounded like he'd said *baby*. Unbelieving, she hobbled over to the door, righted her suitcase, which had fallen, and set it and her guitar case against the wall.

Using the door for support, she peered into the darkness and screamed when Nate loomed up in front of her. He carried a baby seat. The howling she'd mistaken for a cat's yowls had turned to faint whimpers.

"My God. Hurry," she urged him. "A baby!

What if I hadn't heard him crying?" She slowly followed Nate to the couch, where he set the carrier down. "Poor thing, he's shivering. And look how red his skin is."

"Hypothermia. Get him out of the seat and his clothes," Nate ordered. "Put him inside your shirt and wrap up in the fleece. Don't rub his skin. I'll get the fire going."

Michelle sat down and pulled a damp blue blanket away to get at the straps holding the baby in the seat. Quiet now, eyes closed, the infant shook so hard the seat moved. A dingy white cap covered the child's head, but he wore no socks and his thin outfit offered little protection against the elements, including his own blanket.

Next she unbuttoned her pink-and-purple plaid flannel shirt and pulled her T-shirt from her jeans. Her heart broke as she lifted the tiny body, quickly stripped him down to his diaper and then cuddled him to her chest under her shirt. Teeth chattering at the chill he brought with him, she wrapped them both in the warm fleece blanket.

"His hands and feet are freezing cold," she reported, happy to see the fire going. Already the room felt warmer. "How could anyone leave a baby out in a storm like that? It's inhumane."

"Yes, it is." Ice dripped from the words as Nate came to stand over her. "It's neglect and child endangerment. I hope you have a good lawyer."

CHAPTER TWO

"THAT's not funny." Glaring up into the sheriff's cold gray eyes, Michelle carefully shifted the baby so his nose wasn't pressed into her.

"It's not meant to be." He tapped his badge. "I don't joke about the law."

"And I don't abandon defenseless babies."

"No, you just break into houses."

"It's my house," she reminded him through gritted teeth. "So there's no reason I wouldn't have brought the baby inside."

"You knew it was a boy," he said, arms braced across his broad chest.

"A guess from the blue blanket. And it hasn't been substantiated yet. You called him a boy, too."

"He arrived at the same time you did."

"You don't know what time I got here." She narrowed her eyes at him. "Seems to me he arrived at the same time you did."

How dare he accuse her of such an atrocious act? She fully admitted she looked out for number one. You had to put yourself first when no one else did. But she had a soft spot for kids, got along with them better than a lot of adults.

She narrowed her eyes at him. "And as you're so quick to claim, it's your doorstep." She made a point of pulling open the neck of her shirt and looking from the baby to the man. "I think he has your eyes."

His frown turned ferocious. "That's not my kid."

"Are you sure?" she persisted just to aggravate him. "He looks about three or four months old. Think back about a year, something will come to you."

"There is no possibility the child is mine."

"How can you be so sure? A lot of men have vague memories when it comes to things like this."

"I know."

"Oh, right." She rolled her eyes at his arrogance. *You know.*

"I haven't been with a woman since I moved to River Run." Acknowledgment of what he'd revealed came sharp on the heels of his outburst. "Ah, hell."

"Why?" The word burst from her. Shocked, she ran her gaze over him. "You're not bad-looking and your body is smoking hot."

"I have my reasons, which are none of your business." The grimness of his tone warned her the topic was closed.

"Okay." She valued her own privacy too much to disrespect other people's rights to the same. "We've established he's not mine and not yours, so who is he? Was the seat all that was with him? Was there a diaper bag? Maybe there's a note."

"I'll check." Happy for action, he headed for the door.

While he was gone she went through the seat. She found a pacifier and a soggy piece of paper. She was trying to shake it open when Nate returned with a diaper bag.

"What's that?" he demanded.

"It was in the seat." She handed the paper to him. "I think it's the note we're looking for."

Sitting beside her, he carefully unfolded the paper and spread the note. He took up a good portion of the couch and Michelle would have moved away from the large bulk of him, but she wanted to see the note.

Plus he was warm. And he smelled good.

So instead of sensibly moving away, she scooted closer and peered over his large arm. Pretending not to notice his big hands and the thick width of his wrist, she read the note.

Nate,
This is your cosin Jack. I never wanted a kid. Im too old and I cant take care of him and work. I gotta work to stay outta the joint. Jack talked good about you. He was good to me so Im giving his kid to you. If you don't want him giv him to some body to giv him a good home.

"Well, I'm off the hook. Too bad for you," Michelle muttered. The letter offended her. She knew desperation, knew self-absorption, and she could never abandon a child. She suddenly had new respect for her father, who'd at least accepted the responsibility of raising her.

"Joint?" she sneered.

"She means jail."

"I know what joint means. She's barely

literate, but that's no excuse for abandoning
her baby. How could she give her son away?
What about your cousin Jack? Where is he?"

"Dead."

Oh, man. "I'm sorry. What happened?"

"He was killed in a bar fight five months
ago."

"Oh."

"Don't say it like that." The eyes he turned
on her were grieving. "Like he was a lowlife
drunk. Jack was a nice guy, but he was troubled. He should never have followed me into
the service. Some men aren't meant to be kill-
ers. A stint on the front line messed him up
good, and then they sent him home. But the
damage was done. He began drinking, had a
hard time keeping a job."

Nate rubbed a hand over the back of his
neck. "He was excited about the baby. Becoming a father was the first thing he cared
about in a long time. And then he was gone.
He didn't even get to see his son."

"I'm sorry," she said again, with more feeling this time. It was a sad story. She looked
down at the lump of the baby under her shirt
and thought he had a hard time ahead of him.
She didn't remember her mother, she'd died

when Michelle was two, but she had been loved, coddled during those first formative years. Little Jack didn't even have that.

When she looked up, she found the sheriff watching her.

"You need to call Child Services."

"Why?"

Her eyebrows lifted, giving away her surprise. "So they can come get Jack, of course."

He shook his head. "They'd only try to locate his next of kin, and that's me, so there's no need to call them."

"But you aren't equipped to take care of him."

"No," he said grimly, "but it looks like I have little choice."

"So what does that mean? What are you going to do?"

He shrugged. "Raise him."

She blinked at him. "Just like that?"

"Yeah."

"Wow." What did it say about him that he hadn't even hesitated? That he was honorable? Responsible? Both fit with him being a sheriff. "You're not even going to think about it?"

"My uncle took me in, taught me what it

meant to be a man. Jack was like a brother
to me. Of course I'm going to take care of
his kid."

"That's huge. There aren't many men I
know who would just take a baby in like that."

"Then they aren't men."

That was a pretty tough stance. But after a
moment's thought, Michelle nodded. He was
right. One thing she could say about her dad,
he'd never tried to give her away.

"Do you have to start tonight? Couldn't
you call Child Services to take him until
you move into your new place and get all the
gear you'll need?" How could she work on
the house with a baby around? They required
care and feeding, and quiet.

His hands went to his hips and he shook
his head, his expression forbidding.

"Ms. Ross, if anyone is leaving tonight,
it's you. As it is, you'll be leaving first thing
in the morning. Because this is my place for
the next four months."

"But I need to sell the house. And I need
to make improvements."

"Not my problem."

"But it's my house."

"And I have a lease. We've been over this."

"But—"

He held up a hand. "There are rental laws. Read them. Then we'll talk."

Michelle wanted to bite the offending hand. Arrogant jerk. It wasn't her fault her father rented the place without letting her know. She had the right to move on with her life and selling this house was a big part of that.

But she was smart enough to know pressing the issue wouldn't gain her any points, so she retreated.

She nodded at the note. "What about the mother? She didn't sign the note. Do you know her?"

"I met her. Wasn't impressed." The very flatness of his tone spoke volumes. "She has a criminal record so she won't get another chance to hurt Jack."

"Understand I have no sympathy for the woman, but it's possible she knocked. We were arguing and the storm is loud."

"Then she should have knocked harder—" there was no give in his response "—waited for me to open the door and talked to me."

"You might have said no."

"That's no excuse."

"No, but it's a possibility she wasn't willing to risk. Wait…" Michelle suddenly noticed something was different. "He's stopped shivering. I heard that's bad."

"Maybe not." His calm response took the edge off her panic. "If he were still in the cold, yes. But he's been warming up. The need to shiver is gone. Is he still breathing?"

She froze, worried for a moment he'd stopped, but she felt the soft heat of his breath against her chest.

"Yeah." She glanced down at her misshaped T-shirt. "I'd feel better if I could see him."

Nate stepped over, grabbed the neck of her undershirt in both hands and effortlessly tore an eight-inch rip down the front. Michelle gasped, shocked by his outrageous action.

"Hey!" she protested, glowering at him.

"You said you wanted to see the baby. Now you can."

Yeah, and the swell of her breasts and the pink lace of her bra. She pulled her flannel shirt closed over herself and the baby.

"I thought the point was to keep the baby warm."

"Right. And skin-to-skin is the best way. Warm fluids would be good, too."

She nodded toward the diaper bag. "There's probably stuff to make a bottle in there. Do you think you can handle it or should we trade places?"

"If I'm going to raise him, I may as well learn how to feed him now." He grabbed a bottle and a tin of formula from the diaper bag and headed for the kitchen.

Michelle frowned after him. Most people would probably find that admirable. She just found it annoying. It was just as much a fault to have to do everything yourself as to want everyone else to do it for you.

Then again she may just be reacting to her disappointment in not getting to see the baby pressed to Nate's bare chest.

She imagined it would be a pretty impressive sight.

Thinking about it, she decided, no, her annoyance had nothing to do with being denied an erotic peek and everything to do with Sheriff Nate Connor being an arrogant pain in the butt.

In the kitchen Nate leaned against the counter and curled his shaking hands into fists.

How righteous he sounded when he told her he'd be raising Jack. Little did she know the internal fight he went through.

What did he know about raising a kid? Nothing. Sure his uncle had taken him in, but he'd been a stupid teenager and Uncle Stan already had a kid, so taking on Nate had been nothing new. And the Lord knew Nate was already messed up so there was little Uncle Stan could do to damage him.

Not so with Jack. He was an infant with his whole life spread out before him. The damage Nate could do encompassed everything from the baby's health to his spiritual upraising. Nate groaned. Hell, he couldn't remember the last time he went to church, the last time he'd done more than take the Lord's name in vain.

New rule—no cursing.

Because he was a father now, no matter how freaked the notion made him. Because he was no coward and no quitter. He owed Uncle Stan and Jack, so Nate reached for the can of formula and began to read.

He would learn and he would adjust. And he and baby Jack would be just fine.

* * *

The baby stirred against Michelle and she looked down into frowning gray eyes. Jack was awake.

"Hey, little guy, how are you doing?" She smiled in relief and to assure him she was a friend. His color had improved and she cuddled him close and rubbed a finger over the downy softness of wispy wheat-colored hair. "Are you feeling better?"

He blinked at her, which she took as a yes.

"Bad news, buddy, your mom, the low-life witch—" Michelle's sweet tone never changed as she dealt the insult "—dropped you on Cousin Nate's doorstep in the middle of the biggest storm of the season."

He stared at her with sober eyes, taking in every word she spoke.

"Hopefully, your daddy was smarter than your mommy." She nodded at the alertness in his gaze. "The good news is your cousin Nate says he's going to raise you." Chewing the inside of her cheek, she sighed. "Actually, I'm not going to lie to you. It's a good news-bad news thing. He'll be a rock for you, but he'll have impossible expectations. At least that's how it was with my dad."

His little face crumpled and he began to whimper.

"Oh, shoot." Michelle gently bounced Jack, trying to calm him. "No, baby, don't cry. Shh. Maybe I'm wrong. Maybe Nate is different."

"Different from what?" a deep voice demanded.

Flinching internally, she carefully controlled her expression when she met Nate's challenging gaze.

"I was warning him how difficult it can be to live with a sheriff."

He lifted one dark brow, silent reproach in the gesture. "Thanks for undermining me before I've even met the kid."

"The truth is the truth."

"Being sheriff is what I do." He handed her the full bottle. "It's not who I am."

"I was raised by a lawman." The warm bottle felt good in her hand. She checked the temperature of the formula on her wrist. Perfect, of course. She fed it to Jack, who latched onto the nipple and sucked, his little hands coming up to rest on the bottle. "I know what wearing that uniform means. Long hours, community service, duty first. Family a far and distant second."

"You don't know anything about me. I won't be judged by the actions of another."

"Fine. Prove me wrong."

"I would." Nate settled into the corner of the couch. "But you won't be around to see. You just want to sell this house and head back to the city."

He was right. And she wouldn't apologize for wanting to move forward with her life. "I'm not going back to San Francisco. I'm moving to Los Angeles."

"Really?" He lifted one dark brow. "Following some guy south?"

She snorted. As if she'd move across town for some guy. "My agent thinks it'll be better for my songwriting career. And now who's judging?"

"I'm just calling it as I see it."

"There's nothing in this town for me anymore."

"You've never believed there was anything here for you," he said.

Michelle glanced up from the sweet baby to study the stoic sheriff. How did he know her so well when they'd only met briefly at the funeral before today? She didn't think Dad had been the type to talk about his absent daughter. Maybe she'd been wrong about that.

"You were wrong then and you're wrong now."

"Wrong?" Could he read minds now?

"About what the town has to offer."

"I don't have anything in common with the people here. I want more."

"More what?"

The same question her dad had always had for her. She didn't know! She just knew this town lacked what she needed.

"More everything. More music, more options, more money, more entertainment, more men, more people who want more."

And Dad had never understood, never accepted how important music was to her, that songwriting wasn't just a dream but what drove her.

"Shallow. I guess you're right after all. River Run has character, people with heart and integrity who care about their neighbors, where life is more important than entertainment and meeting strangers in the street."

No surprise, Sheriff Nate Connor didn't understand, either. Why that hurt she couldn't say.

She ran the back of her finger over baby

Jack's powder-soft cheek, wishing him a better life in River Run than she'd had. "He's asleep again."

"Good. Hypothermia is hard on the system."

"Is the storm going to get better or worse tomorrow?"

"Why? You have somewhere you gotta be?" he mocked her.

"Just answer the question."

"Worse. This was only supposed to be a light snow flurry, but a massive cold front pushed down from Alaska causing blizzard conditions. It's supposed to get worse before it gets better. We've battened down the town and advised people to stay inside except for emergencies."

Nodding, she tucked the fleece-wrapped baby in the crook of the couch and set his bottle on the oak coffee table.

"Then I should get at least one of my other suitcases tonight." She reached for her shoes.

Nate didn't move. "You're not going out in the storm. Didn't you hear me say I advised the townspeople to stay inside?"

"This is an emergency."

"You're safe and sound inside a warm

house. There's food and water, and a flush-
ing toilet. How is this an emergency?"

His long-suffering expression made her grit
her teeth.

"I need clothes. I have a change of under-
wear in my overnight case, but not clothes."
She tugged at her ripped T-shirt. "And the
ones I have on came into contact with a
Neanderthal."

"You can borrow something of mine." He
shrugged off her sarcasm. "Nobody is going
back out into the storm."

Shooting daggers at him, because she'd
hoped he'd offer to get the cases for her, she
made her way around the table to the middle
of the room. Her ankle throbbed but held her
weight.

"Ten minutes ago you were ready to send
me on my way."

"That was before I'd been back outside.
The storm has worsened."

"All the more reason to go now. I'm going
to get my suitcase and you can't stop me."

He laughed. And pushed to his feet with
a lithe grace that spoke of muscle and disci-
pline and the easy strength to make her do
anything he wanted her to.

Aggravating man.

"You don't scare me." Still she couldn't prevent taking an instinctive step back. And immediately felt her ankle turn. Pain streaked through her foot and she started to fall.

She screamed.

The baby cried.

And the lights went out.

CHAPTER THREE

"I'VE got you." Nate caught a bundle of soft female curves in his arms. She smelled of something fruity, clean and tart...and good enough to eat.

Too bad she was prickly as a porcupine. Because it looked as if he was stuck with her for a couple of days.

"I'm fine." She twisted against him, seeking release. "You've made your point. I'm not going outside."

"Stay still." He shifted his hold from her arms to her waist, practically spanning the narrow width with his hands. She was tinier than he'd thought. "You're going to hurt yourself worse than you already have."

"The baby is crying."

"We'll get to Jack in a minute." For some reason Nate couldn't let Michelle go. She'd untucked her shirt when she stuck the baby under the hem and the thumb of his right hand rested on the silky warmth of her skin. It wasn't personal, he assured himself. It wasn't Michelle he wanted.

It just felt so good to hold a woman in his arms.

But he had enough common sense to know the landlord who wanted to sell his house out from under him was not the place to kickstart his libido.

He had no choice but to let her stay for a couple of days, but after that she'd be gone. Either to a place in town or preferably back to the city to stay until his lease ended and she could return to do her thing without his bumping into her.

She stopped struggling, going totally still. The lights were out but the fire gave off enough light for him to realize the dark shook her.

He could handle a woman's tears. When your mother cried at the drop of a hat, you learned to cope or became an emotional wreck yourself. Still the long day—days— and the baby must have him off his game, because he really didn't want to see the tears sparkling in Michelle's emerald-bright eyes fall. Already he knew enough about her to know she'd hate putting on a tearful display for him.

"What's wrong, Michelle? Are you afraid of the dark?"

Anger instantly sparked, wiping the distress from her face, replacing it with haughty distain.

"Of course not." Her chin lifted and instead of pulling away from him she stepped forward until her pink flannel shirt brushed against the khaki of his uniform. "I'm at my best in the dark."

His body reacted with a rush. Holy sh— Moly.

Ding! Ding! Ding! Round one to Michelle.

A warrior knew the advantages of a timely retreat. He quickly released her and took two steps back, narrowly missing the coffee table and a fall of his own.

She flipped her hair and flashed him a glance of triumph as she moved to pick up the baby and coo at him. Not a tear in sight, and she seemed to have forgotten her missing suitcases.

Mission accomplished. So it hadn't been a total defeat.

"Good. Then keep an eye on Jack. I'm going to go get some flashlights and candles. Plus I have to make some calls. I may be a few minutes."

"Okay." But she couldn't prevent a flinch of uncertainty.

"Don't let the fire go out."

"Don't worry."

"I'll be as fast as I can and we'll get some light in here."

"Thanks. I think the dark upsets Jack."

Nate stared down at Jack held snuggly in her arms and an unexpected rush of emotion swelled up in him. The baby had Nate's uncle's eyes, the resemblance especially strong with Jack scowling like he was doing now.

How Nate had loved that old man.

Funny, he'd always thought of Uncle Stan as old, but hell, at forty-two his uncle had only been ten years older than Nate was now when he took in a wild fourteen-year-old.

He'd been in a bad place but Uncle Stan took no guff from him. There'd been no bluff in the man, but he'd cared. He'd been as free with his affections as he'd been with his disciplines. Nate had needed both.

He'd learned how a real man acted.

How proud Uncle Stan would be of baby Jack. Though it hurt Nate to admit it, he was glad his uncle hadn't seen Jack Sr.'s spiral into drunken obscureness. He wouldn't have blamed Nate—Stan believed a man was responsible for his own choices—but it would have killed him to see Jack's pain, and the weakness that took him over.

The baby, the continuance of the Connor family, would have thrilled Uncle Stan. Michelle was surprised by Nate's willingness to take the baby on, but Nate owed Uncle Stan and Jack too much, loved them too much, to shame them by turning away baby Jack.

Which meant for the time being he needed Michelle. At least for tonight; beyond that, he'd see.

"Right." He mocked her claim that Jack was the one afraid of the dark.

She hit him with a scorching glare, but all she said, was "Food would be good, too."

Her bravado and the underlying vulnerability got to him. He called himself a chump but once he'd gathered the flashlights, candles and a battery lantern he returned to the living room.

He lit candles and placed them on the mantel, handed her a flashlight and set the blazing lantern on the coffee table. But it was her smile that lit up the room.

"Double chump," he muttered as he escaped to the kitchen. The phones were out, too, so he used his cell to call the county supervisor's office to get the status of the utilities. He learned the storm had taken out several major hubs. And then the line went dead as his phone beeped and informed him he was out of service.

"Great."

The need to fix the problems pressed at him, but there was literally nothing he could do except prepare for the cold night ahead. The loss of electricity meant they'd have no working heater.

He grabbed a box from the utility room and piled in his stash from the refrigerator and cupboard, tossed in utensils and topped it with plates, mugs, a pan and napkins. Next he used the flashlight he'd kept to find two sleeping bags in the attached garage.

Why he bothered to go to so much trouble for a woman so self-absorbed she rarely contacted the father who obviously adored her, Nate didn't know. And sure she was watching the baby, but she hadn't even offered to help. No doubt she expected to be waited on hand and foot. Well, that wouldn't wash here. He expected people to pull their own weight and since her temporary stay was on his dime, she'd just have to meet his expectations.

He frowned, remembering what he'd overheard her telling Jack. That kids of sheriffs had to live with high expectations and little freedom. It made him recall the early days with his uncle Stan. That's exactly how he'd felt. The restrictions had chafed badly, but it had also felt good to know someone cared about where he was and what he was doing. To have someone who checked up on him and made sure he had something to eat.

It took two trips to get everything to the living room and Michelle was sitting on the hearth pawing through the food box when he came back with the sleeping bags.

"Big boy, you are my hero." The sultry look of anticipation on her face made him wish she were gazing at him instead of the stew she was transferring from plastic container to cast-iron pot. "I'm starved, and this smells really good."

When she put her finger in her mouth to

clean off a smudge of gravy, he had to disguise a groan with a cough.

That brought her attention up from the food.

"You're not catching a cold, are you?"

Was that real concern in her voice?

"Because you're a parent now, you have to take better care of yourself."

Nate rolled his eyes. He should have known better.

"Thanks for your concern." The sarcasm slid off his tongue before he could rein it in. Damn, now he'd have to put up with the sulks for an hour while she pouted around. He moderated his tone. "But I'm fine."

Unoffended, she flashed him a dimpled grin. "I'm just saying. No more wandering around in the cold without a jacket."

Surprised by her easy response, Nate felt some of the tension in his shoulders lessen. Maybe the woman had a few redeeming qualities.

"Yes, Mother."

"Oh." Her green eyes widened and then narrowed dangerously. "You didn't go there."

He had. And her huff made him add, "You

want a cap and slippers to go with that advice?"

"You're going to pay for that, buster." She promised retribution. "Now you get to play chef."

She pushed the heavy pot into the flames of the fire. And to punctuate her point she stood, dusted off her curvy butt and hobbled back to the couch, where she claimed her seat in the corner. Arms crossed over her chest plumped up her breasts, pushing pink lace and considerable cleavage into view.

"I like it steaming hot," she said with a slow lick of her lips.

Oh, devious, devious woman. The wanton knew exactly how to make a man pay. And it had nothing to do with cooking supper.

Determined to keep his composure, he put his back to the tempting sight of the contrary female.

"You're fickle, Ms. Ross. First I'm your hero, then I'm a sorry fellow tasked with heating your stew."

He glanced over his shoulder, taking in the cozy scene backlit by the encompassing darkness. Baby sleeping, a tiny blanket-wrapped bundle; smug woman, pretty in pink flannel.

As she caught his gaze, she flipped her hair in a gesture no doubt learned in the cradle. The long tresses looked like flowing gold in the firelight.

"Cooked steaming hot," he emphasized.

She lifted a brow. "I wasn't talking about the stew."

Michelle bit back a laugh. She swore the man almost swallowed his tongue.

Served him right. Calling her *mother*. The nerve.

Stew was good, though. As if on cue, her stomach growled. Not loud enough to be heard, thank goodness, but a definite reminder it had been close to nine hours since she last ate.

"But it'll do for now," she purred, taking satisfaction in seeing his shoulders brace as if ready for a fight. Better prepare, big boy, she was here to fight for her inheritance, and she wouldn't let a massive he-man stand in her way.

Flirting came as natural to her as breathing. And if a little harmless seduction threw him off his stride, good. It might get her what she wanted and no way would she fall for River Run's newest lawman.

"You'll mind your manners if you want a serving," he calmly responded.

Ah. A challenge.

"You'd really deny an injured woman a simple meal?" she chastised in a wounded voice, soft and just a little accusatory.

He just shook his head without turning and dished up two bowls of the savory stew. Then he opened a foil-wrapped loaf of bread and cut two big slices, putting one in each of the bowls. Walking over, he handed one of the bowls to her.

"Thank you." She reached eagerly for the meal, too hungry to pretend otherwise. The first bite tasted divine and she moaned in pleasure. "Excellent. Did you make this?"

"No," he said from the brown corduroy recliner next to her. "A friend cooked it for me." He eyed her over his steaming bowl. "You're going to be trouble."

It wasn't a question, but she nodded. She didn't usually reveal her weaknesses, especially to strong competitors, but weariness and desperation drove her to the point of honesty.

"I need to stay here," she said bravely.

"And if I say no?"

She chewed carefully, the yummy stew suddenly sitting heavy in her stomach. "You can't."

"We both know I should."

"I don't know that," she denied. "I think we can help each other out here."

That stopped him midbite. He lifted one dark eyebrow. "How's that?"

"I need a place to stay." She choked out the words, then cleared her throat and put determination in the rest. "And you need help with little Jack."

"Hmm. Seems I could hire someone who won't cause trouble to do that."

"But you don't have to pay me." Hmm. "Much."

He laughed. A hearty, rusty-sounding bark that came from deep inside him and startled the baby awake.

Michelle immediately reached for the baby, her first instinct to soothe and settle him, and then her healthy sense of self-preservation kicked in. So instead she cooed to little Jack on her way to handing him to Nate.

Let him see what he'd be dealing with without in-house assistance.

"Here you go." She held the crying child out to Nate.

"Humph." He set his bowl on the coffee table and took the squalling baby into his arms.

The trick worked because the baby continued to cry no matter what Nate did to soothe him. Then she felt bad because Jack refused to be mollified. Nate patted him, talked to him, put him over his shoulder and held him in his lap. Actually he was very good with the baby, holding him well and confidently.

But nothing made Jack happy.

Once she finished eating she set her dishes aside and took him so Nate could finish his meal.

She thought she'd be able calm the child, even hummed a little song for him, which seemed to be working and then it wasn't. Instead he worked himself into a full screaming fit. So much for her plan. And her ego.

"I changed his diaper," she said even as she checked him again to make sure he was still dry. "And he just had a bottle. I don't know why he's so upset."

"Maybe he's still hungry," Nate offered. "Do you think he'd like some stew?"

"He's too small to eat that. Or any solids. How old did you say he was?"

"Four months."

Did that mean Jack could have food? She wasn't sure. "I don't know. I had a coworker with a new baby. I think she started feeding her little girl about this age. But if so, it was only soft cereal or pureed fruits and vegetables."

"Yeah, well, we don't have any of that. I'm going to give him a little of the broth."

Michelle hesitated, still unsure, but the frantic crying wore at her nerves. At this point she was willing to give it a try. She gratefully released the baby into Nate's care.

"Be careful," she urged him. "Make sure you don't get any chunks of food. And don't give him too much. It's rich and his system won't be used to it."

"Let's see if he even likes it." Nate dipped the tip of his spoon in the thick broth and brought it to the shrieking baby's mouth, touching the tiny tongue with a small taste. For a moment there was no change, but Nate tried it again. This time the crying stuttered as Jack worked his tongue against his lips, but his little body still shuddered with the force of his sobs.

"That's promising." Nate fed him another small sip.

"Not too fast," she cautioned as blessed silence surrounded them.

"He likes it."

"I'm sure he does. It's got more flavor than anything else he's ever eaten."

"It shut him up." Nate sent her a superior look as he continued to feed the baby. "You can't argue with the results."

"I can if he gets sick later," she shot back. "I think that's enough."

"Okay. One more." He talked to the baby, explained this was the last bite, but he could have another bottle later. And Nate continued to talk to Jack after he lifted him to his shoulder, telling him about the storm and how Jack had to do his part to help them all have a good night under the trying circumstances.

He talked until Jack fell asleep.

"Good job." She applauded. "Hopefully he's out for a while."

"I guess it's too much to hope he's out for the night?"

"Afraid so. Speaking of which, who gets

him for the night? Are you ready to agree to my terms?"

He sighed, the baby lifting and falling with the movement of his broad chest. "Trouble with a capital *T*."

She grinned at the resignation in his voice. "Just saying. Life will be so much easier with me around."

"Huk."

What kind of noise was that?

"You okay?" She couldn't tell if he was choking or trying not to laugh. Maybe a little of both?

He reprimanded her with the flash of diamond-sharp eyes as he fought to get himself under control.

"Witch. Lucky for me I don't need to make a decision tonight." He nodded at a couple of sleeping bags she hadn't noticed before. "We'll be sleeping together down here next to the fire."

CHAPTER FOUR

MICHELLE'S spine snapped straight. "What do you mean sleep together? Why do we have to sleep down here?"

"The heater is electric," Nate stated calmly. "That means there's no heat upstairs."

"Surely we'd be warm enough under our blankets? I don't remember sleeping down here as a kid."

"Your dad told me he changed from gas to electric some years ago. Probably felt it was safer." He stood and set the baby in the seat. "But if you want to try finding enough blankets to huddle under, be my guest. Jack and I are sleeping down here next to the fire."

As if he cared less what she chose to do, he gathered the dirty dishes and pot of stew and carried it all into the kitchen.

Obviously no help would be coming from that direction. Michelle bit her lip and eyed the distance to the stairs. The twelve feet seemed daunting enough considering her foot had given out when she'd barely passed the coffee table before the lights went out. Add in the stairs and the walk down the hall while carrying her overnight bag and gathering extra blankets along the way, and she saw the impossibility of the challenge.

"I'll sleep on the couch," she announced when Nate returned to the room.

"Suit yourself." He offered no argument. But he stood and surveyed her with his hands braced on his hips. "It'll be a little lumpy once I remove the mattress from the Hide-A-Bed, but you can keep the cushions."

Though it seemed an obvious question, she didn't ask why he didn't just pull out the Hide-A-Bed and use it as is. He'd already stated his intent to be close to the fire.

Plus she didn't want to share a bed with Nate Connor. He was too big, too gruff, too dominating to share such a small space with. There'd be no getting away from him.

She could still feel the imprint of his body on hers, remember the taste of him on her tongue. The memories made sharing a bed with him too tempting and way too dangerous.

Nope, not going there. The couch made total sense. She wouldn't have to walk up the stairs. She'd be near the fire. And she'd have the necessary distance from the sexy but aggravating sheriff.

Her game plan set, she glanced up to see Nate zipping the two sleeping bags together.

"Hey, I need one of those over here."

"Nope," he said without looking up. "I'm too big to share one sleeping bag with the baby."

Measuring the width of his shoulders, she really couldn't argue with the statement. "Then he can sleep with me."

"Nope." He finished with the bags and draped them over the back of the chair. Next he picked up the heavy coffee table and easily moved it across the room, opening up the space in front of the fire. Then he turned toward the couch. "I'm going to need you to move."

"Why not?" She held out a hand, silently asking for assistance in rising.

"Because you're going to get cold and end up down on the mattress with us." He grasped her hand and pulled her to her feet.

She practically flew off the couch, ending

up way too close to him. She looked into his eyes, pretended to be unaffected by the show of strength. The man was solid as a rock and warm as sun-baked stone.

"That seems easy to predict since you won't give me a sleeping bag." Making no attempt to move out of his way, she lazily twirled a strand of hair around her finger. "I'm disappointed in you, Nate. Trying to maneuver me into sleeping with you on our first date."

A ferocious scowl crashed over his brow, making him look like an angry lion.

"Woman, are you crazy? We're snowed in. We are not, nor will we ever be, dating."

"Really?" she challenged in a totally reasonable tone. "I cooked for you. You revealed your sexual history. And we necked on the couch. Sounds like a date to me."

His glower intensified through her recitation. "You *are* insane."

"Maybe." She shrugged, pleased at riling him. "But I'm not easy. You're going to have to work harder than that to get me between the sleeping bags."

He cringed.

Not a great reaction for her ego, but she

didn't let it show. And it had been a bad pun.
"Can you at least find me some blankets?"

He wanted to say no, his reluctance was
written all over him. But he picked up a flashlight and turned for the stairs. The noise an-
nouncing his annoyance would have been a
huff coming from a woman, but it was too
low and rough to be considered anything
other than a growl.

Rather than take the chance that his temper would have him tossing the cushions beyond her reach, she removed them and set
them beside the couch. She tried to pull out
the bed but couldn't get good purchase with
her bad foot.

Jack stirred so she lifted him, sat and
hummed softly until he settled into sleep
again.

Nate returned with a large navy blue comforter and a couple of pillows. He dropped
everything on the far side of the room and
came to stand over her.

"How's he doing?" For all their differences,
Jack represented neutral ground.

"He's restless," she said quietly, hoping
not to disturb the sleeping baby. "I'm sure
he misses his mom."

"He's going to have to get over that." Nate's tone was grim.

"So you don't think she'll be back? She may not be much of a mother, but she's all he's ever known."

"If she has any smarts at all, she better not show up here. If I see her again, I'll press charges for child endangerment. Which reminds me, I need you to write out a statement."

Michelle shrank from the idea. It spoke of an involvement she preferred to stay away from. But Jack's welfare demanded she do the right thing.

"Can it wait until the morning? I'm wiped."

He gave one short nod. "I guess. Let's get these beds put together."

He made short work of it, easily pulling out the Hide-A-Bed and stripping off the mattress then folding it back up and putting the cushions back in place.

Considering his grouchiness she watched in wonder as he brought over the comforter, draped it in half over the couch and tossed a pillow on the end away from the fire. Next he placed the mattress vertically in front of the fire and spread out the doubled-up sleeping bags.

When the beds were done, he came for Jack.

"I'm sure you remember where the bathroom is," he mentioned as he rose from placing the baby between the sleeping bags.

She nodded but lost track of the comment when he stripped off his shirt, giving her the view she'd missed earlier. She'd been right—he was ripped. *Impressive* was too mild a word for how fine he looked.

She was so distracted she failed to notice his hands move toward his belt buckle.

"Weren't you headed to the bathroom?" he demanded.

"What?" She took in his stance and grinned. "Don't mind me. I'm not shy," she assured him. "But since you appear to be, I'll respect your sensibilities."

Picking up her suitcase, she limped toward the hall. A sigh sounded behind her, and then a large hand took the case from her and Nate disappeared down the hall, his broad shoulders shadowed against the light he carried. He turned through a door and the light dimmed.

Her hero yet again. How could she have forgotten a light?

The man had such a protective streak she was no longer surprised he'd taken on Jack so easily. He returned so quickly she had no time to step out of his way. Suddenly she found herself pressed up against all that gorgeous skin.

Oh, my. Warm and hard, he felt so good she wanted to melt into all that masculine heat. He must have taken time somewhere along the line to wash up because he smelled yummy. She recognized the smell of his soap from the throw she'd been wrapped up in earlier. It was even better on his heated skin.

"Mmm. You do smell good." She restrained the urge to lick the hard pecs in front of her. Instead she lifted her gaze to his. "Almost good enough to make me forget my vow to never get involved with a man in law enforcement."

"You tempt me, Ms. Ross." Long-fingered hands wrapped around her waist and lifted her into the air. He turned so they traded places, and then he let her feet touch the ground. But rather than release her, he bent over her, his lips just an inch away from hers. His minty breath was an enticing invitation that whispered over her skin. She was about to meet him halfway, when he shifted his head to speak in her ear. "But it's best if we don't complicate this relationship more than necessary."

"Complicated doesn't scare me," she bluffed.

Okay, that felt a little too real. Maybe she needed to dial it back a bit.

Why encourage him when she agreed with his decree? Starting something with anyone in River Run smacked of stupidity. Starting something with the sheriff would be a mistake of major proportions.

He lifted a dark brow as he straightened. "That's because you don't stick around for the complications."

"Ouch!" She flinched, exaggerating her hurt to hide the pain. "That's just mean."

"Sometimes the truth hurts."

"Indeed. But I have to wonder. Is your fear of complications responsible for your long dry spell? Are you a simple man, Sheriff?"

"Give the lady a prize." He mocked her. "I spend my days solving problems and keeping order. When I get home, I want peace and quiet, not to juggle the needs and demands of three different women and their well-meaning friends and relatives."

"Ah." She nodded sagely but made no effort to hide the glee in her eyes. "Now I understand. A virile, strong-bodied man like you comes to town unattached. The matchmakers probably swarmed all over you."

She tapped her finger against her lips as she contemplated him. "Which means one of two things happened. Either you accepted their cleverly casual offers for a home-cooked meal and found yourself set up with a number of lovely companions eager to follow up with a date. And you made the mistake of trying to juggle the women while you figured out who you really wanted to date. Or you saw the minefield ahead of you and decided not to risk precious body parts by alienating matchees. Or matchmakers."

"You can laugh, but I'm rather fond of all my body parts."

She grinned. "I imagine you are. My guess is it was the former. There are a lot of nice ladies with single relatives in town."

"So there are." He chucked her under the

chin. "No need to blow your vow now. Use all the soap you want."

With that he closed the door in her face.

She blinked at the wooden barrier. Oh, he wasn't getting away with that. She wasn't through playing with him yet. She yanked the door open and stepped into the hall. Nate was at the end and before she could challenge him he turned. Light flowed over his broad back, highlighting a vivid scar running from his left collarbone across his shoulder blade and under his arm.

It was a shocking blight on the perfect canvas of his muscular body. Between one thundering heartbeat and another she knew he would hate for her to mention it. Wouldn't want to talk about it.

Here was his reason for keeping to himself.

She remembered her dad telling her his new deputy sheriff had been in the army, that he'd been a Ranger or something. Everything she knew about special forces told her his body was a weapon. Which probably told her why he was a sheriff in Podunk River Run instead of still fighting the good fight.

As a woman who knew the value of beauty, she understood his inclination to hide the imperfection. And she respected his right to privacy.

She retreated into the bathroom and closed the door.

Wrapped in Nate's throw, Michelle cuddled under the comforter, clenching her teeth to keep them from chattering. It galled her big-time, but Nate had been right. The couch sat under the window. And the distance from the fire was too great to offset the icy glass over her.

Giving in, she gathered her covers and her pillow and used the dim light of the fire to make her way to the middle of the room and the cozy bed where Jack and Nate slept.

Just being closer to the fire helped and she eyed the makeshift bed, wondering if there was a way she could join them without waking Nate. Hearing him gloat was the last thing she wanted at two in the morning.

He slept on his back and easily took up half the space on the mattress. Jack slept about a foot to the left of Nate, which left about eighteen inches for Michelle to squeeze into.

No way she could climb into the sleeping bag without waking both males so she wouldn't even try. She set the pillow down next to Jack, drew the comforter around herself and, trying for stealth, lay down on the edge of the mattress.

She sighed, but before her head even hit the pillow, Nate erupted into action.

He leaped over Jack, caught her around the middle and rolled with her. Comforter and pillow went flying. Instinctively Michelle threw her arms up in self-defense.

Nate blocked the move, caught her right arm, twisted and flipped her. She screamed, in pain and fright.

The baby began to cry.

"Nate." She spit out carpet fibers and called his name. "Nate, it's me—Michelle."

"Michelle?"

The weight he used to contain her shifted, tensing then relaxing, and suddenly the fight went out of him and he sprawled full-length over her body. He went into a rant of creative and foul curses.

"Hell, woman, are you insane? I'm a soldier. You can't sneak up on me when I'm sleeping. I could have broken your neck."

"My neck is fine. But you may break something else if you don't move," she wheezed out, no longer nervous. "Can I have my arm back? Please."

"Good Lord." Two hands appeared on either side of her and his weight disappeared. A moment later, he flipped her again, gently this time, and his hands ran lightly over her, checking for injuries. "I'm sorry. Are you hurt? Where?"

"Nate. Stop." She grabbed his hands and held them still. She couldn't get her breath back with his hands on her. "I'm fine. You were right. I got cold and moved to the mattress. I didn't mean to startle you."

"Right." He scrubbed his face. Glanced at Jack, who'd been jostled awake by Nate's abrupt departure from the bed, and then back at her. "Look, some habits die hard. Do me a favor, next time announce you're joining me in bed."

"Next time?" She swallowed hard. "You are feeling lucky."

His eyebrows drew together as he processed her comment while clearly still shaken. He shook his head. "Smart-ass."

"What can I say? You bring out the best in me."

"Jack's crying and I'm freezing my butt off. Let's go to bed."

Currently her body was overheated from proximity to him. Maybe she should rethink the whole sleeping-together thing?

No, then he'd know she was running scared.

She allowed him to help her to her feet. She grabbed the crying baby, singing softly to soothe him, while Nate straightened the bedding.

Wrapping the throw around the baby, she watched with interest as Nate unzipped the sleeping bags.

"Why are you unlinking them?"

"With the extra body heat and the comforter we don't need the additional warmth."

"And with the three of us it would be a tad cozy?"

He lifted one bare shoulder, let it drop. "Yeah, there's that."

"Good plan."

"I thought so." He nodded toward Jack. "He's probably hungry. Christy was still taking a bottle at night at that age."

"Christy? You have a daughter?"

His head whipped around and there was

no sign of sleep in the gaze that cut through her. "Christy is my friend's daughter. He died in combat."

"And you came to River Run to check up on her?" The guy really did have an overactive protective gene.

"Something like that." He was defensive.

Telling herself it was none of her business, Michelle expressed sorrow over the loss of his friend and asked if he'd get the bottle for Jack.

While he went to the kitchen to clean the bottle, she and Jack got settled on the mattress. The baby continued to fuss until Nate finished making the bottle with the water he had warming by the fire.

She concentrated on Jack, paying no attention as Nate joined them in the bed. Right, as if she could ignore a six-foot-three-inch mass of muscle and testosterone. But she was determined to pretend nonchalance.

He settled against his pillow with a sigh.

Jack put his tiny hand on Nate's biceps, and Michelle could swear he sighed, too.

She turned on her side, facing the baby, and plumped up her pillow. Her eyes blinked as she slid her feet over the cool nylon of the sleeping bag. She focused on the bottle, saw it was almost gone. Her feet encountered a firm, warm surface. She sighed and slid into sleep.

Nate sat up to burp Jack and felt Michelle's toes dig into his calf as she moved with him. Sound asleep, she had an innocence about her that belied her tough exterior. And drew him far more than he could afford.

The truth was he found too much about her way too tempting. He dismissed her bravado; saw it for the shield it was. Some might see her aggression as manipulation and her flippancy as fake, but he heard the self-honesty driving it and appreciated the bluntness.

Her patience and connection with Jack awed Nate. He would have been lost without her tonight.

She was beautiful and knew it. Used it. This woman knew games he'd never even heard of. And wanted no part of. High maintenance thy name was Michelle Ross.

She'd been right. He was a simple man, and he wanted a simple life. He'd deal with taking in Jack because he had to, because he was family.

Nate had originally moved here to support his best friend's widow, to watch over his infant daughter. Nate and Kim had been friends for three years. He knew he could count on her help with Jack.

As soon as the storm ended, he'd call Kim; make a date to talk to her about what he needed for Jack.

Now was definitely not the time to let his irrational attraction for Sleeping Beauty sway him from his set path. But as he set the snoozing baby between them and sank back onto his pillow he made no effort to move away from her seeking toes. The human connection felt too good to lose.

His last thought before fading into sleep was a prayer that the storm ended soon. Spending time housebound with a woman he had no business desiring was his idea of torture.

CHAPTER FIVE

THE next two days were absolute torture. Being cooped up with a bear of a man and a traumatized infant did not make for lots of fun.

Luckily Michelle's foot healed up pretty fast and got her off the couch and puttering around between bouts of watching Jack.

Child care was not in her plans when she headed home to sell her dad's house, but poor Jack was miserable. Obviously he missed his mother, plus his experience from the day before had left him with a cold. Bottom line he was unhappy when he was awake and his cold kept him from sleeping more than a few minutes at a time.

She and Nate settled into a grudging truce as they shared baby duty. She thought his patience would run out, but reluctantly acknowledged he held up his end. He'd prop

Jack against his shoulder and go about his business. And he was always busy. He kept the fire going, cooked, cleaned, did dishes, handled the trash.

On the first day, she watched him make tuna sandwiches, mostly one-handed, for lunch and later he did paperwork at his desk. She took the baby, and by the second day he'd devised a sling that helped to leave his hands free.

Because she liked to cook, she helped with the meals and left the rest to him. She spent the remainder of her time wandering through the house taking stock.

She was surprised to find her room remained the same as she'd left it, complete with purple curtains, butterflies, musical notes and pop-star posters.

The house was in good shape, better than she would have thought, but then her dad had always demanded she help out with some new project. From gardening and fixing a broken step to repairing a toilet and building her tree house he'd always had something he needed her help with. She had to admit the fix-it knowledge had come in handy over the years.

And she'd loved her tree house. He'd made

her a castle. They'd built it together the first year she went to Princess Camp. And she'd used it clear through her senior year in high school.

Late the second day she followed Nate up to the attic to see if there was any baby furniture they could use. There wasn't. Her mother might have kept that kind of thing. Her dad got rid of anything they weren't currently using.

What they did find was a very dusty wooden rocking chair. At her insistence Nate carried it down to the garage.

"This is filthy. And one of the arms is warped." He dusted off his hands after setting it down. "The only thing it's good for is firewood."

"We'll see." She bounced Jack on her hip. "Yes, it's dirty but it's sturdy. A little sanding and a good cleaning is all it needs."

He lifted a skeptical brow. "You're on your own there. Speaking of firewood, I have to replenish our supply."

"Okay, let me put my jacket on and I'll help."

"You have Jack." He reached for a hooded coat he kept in the garage. "I can handle it."

"Stubborn man," she muttered as he headed out the back door. She carried Jack into the living room, placed him in the middle of the mattress and piled up a barricade of pillows between him and the hearth. As he'd barely mastered turning over, she figured he couldn't get far in the few minutes it took her to help Nate.

Dragging on her jacket, she arrived back in the garage in time to hold the door open so Nate didn't have to struggle to get it while carrying the large load of wood. A gesture he accepted with a less than gracious grunt.

Rolling her eyes at his back, she stepped out the back door to walk the short distance to the wood shed but a hard hand wrapped around her elbow and pulled her to a stop.

"Stay inside," he insisted. "It's too slick out there for your weak ankle. You'll only end up on your pretty ass."

"Ohh, so you think I have a pretty tush?" She wiggled her butt enticingly. "I think yours is nice, too."

"Nut." He shook his head, but the corner of his mouth quirked up just a little. "Now go back inside. I can do this. What I can't do is take care of Jack and you, too."

"Fine." She flounced around on her heel and promptly felt her foot slide on a frozen patch, going out from under her. Luckily, his hand on her arm kept her from falling.

"Careful." He pulled her close, clamping her to his sturdy frame.

Humor fled as she clung to him. The last thing she needed was to hurt herself worse than she already had, especially when her ankle was still on the mend.

Breathless from the near fall, she gazed up at him. "Thank you."

He picked her up and set her inside the garage door. "Does everything always have to be about sex with you?"

Indignant, her hands went to her hips. "How is 'thank you' about sex?"

"I don't know." He threw his gloved hands up, revealing his frustration. "It's the way you talk, everything sounds sexy."

Well, yeah. Using her sexuality usually got her what she wanted. And okay, she'd admit to an attraction to all that raw masculinity. But he was being far too sensitive. Sometimes "thank you" just meant "thank you." Defensive, she tossed his argument back at him.

"Or maybe it's the way you hear it. I just

came out to help. You're the one who started talking about my ass."

His eyes narrowed in a scowl and he opened his mouth. Then he obviously thought better of it because he closed his mouth with a click of his teeth.

After a deep breath, he said, "Just hold the door. This will only take a few more minutes."

"Yes, sir." She gave him a pert salute.

Looking at the dark clouds and heavy snowfall, she rubbed her hands together for warmth and wished for the storm to end soon.

The attack began with a close-range sniper shot. Nate heard the whining echo as he caught his best friend in his arms. He went down under Quentin's dead weight. Gunfire broke out. Shouts and then screams rent the air. Return mortar fire boomed and the foundation shook.

Nate dragged Quentin inside. Shafts of light were thick with dust and sand. Paper-thin walls offered little protection but Nate bent over Quentin, calling his name, demanding an answer. His heart in his throat, he checked for a pulse and his hand came back bloody.

The building suddenly exploded. Nate threw his body over Quentin. A lancing pain tore through Nate's shoulder. And then everything went black.

Nate sat straight up in bed. The sound of mortar fire rang in his ears. Sweat beaded his brow and he pushed out of the sleeping bag to pace the chilly room. He grabbed a T-shirt to wipe his face, wishing it was that easy to wipe out his memories.

No, that was wrong. Quentin deserved better from Nate.

He'd told Command they needed to change up the routine. A smart soldier knew predictable was deadly. But nothing about the damn war was logical. So the simple changing of the guard had turned bloody. Worse, he'd changed shifts with Quentin. Their positions should have been reversed.

Nate should be dead and Quentin should be with his wife and daughter.

His blood was on Nate's hands. The first shot had killed him and Nate's efforts to shield him from the blast had been worthless and had nearly cost him his arm.

Nate walked to the kitchen, opened the refrigerator and stared at the contents unseeingly.

Quentin had had so little time with his beautiful daughter, Christy, but he'd loved her so much. He never talked about her, as if he wanted to protect her from the vileness of the war and their everyday life. But he showed Nate pictures, would just hand over a stack without a word. And Nate savored every candid shot of the plump little girl with his buddy's nose and hair and her mother's eyes.

Those pictures of home, of an innocent child filled with the joy of life and discovery, were what kept Nate going. When the sand and the heat and the hatred got to be too much, he'd remember Christy's smile and remind himself he was here to make the world a better, safer place for her.

And sometimes he actually believed it.

He closed the refrigerator door and began to pace, the terrazzo tile icy under his bare feet. Wait… He swung back to the refrigerator and pulled the door open. The light was on. Good, the electricity was back. That meant the storm must be abating.

Thank God.

He used to relive the nightmare of that day in his dreams every night. They'd become less frequent over the past year. He knew exactly what brought it on now: his decision to raise Jack.

They'd saved Nate's arm, but his career was over. He hadn't hesitated when he returned stateside—he'd moved to River Run. He owed it to his friend to look after his family. And that's what he'd done for the past three years.

"Are you okay?" Michelle's soft voice came out of the darkness.

He gave a harsh laugh. "Yeah, I'm just fine."

"Couldn't sleep?" She leaned a hip against the counter and crossed one pink polka-dot-socked foot over the other.

"Touch of heartburn from the chili tonight." He pounded his chest for emphasis. It wasn't a total lie; it just wasn't what woke him.

She opened a cupboard and tossed him a bottle of antacids. "Sorry. I like spicy. Next time I'll go lighter on the jalapeños."

"No," he said, sorry he'd picked on her food. "Don't." He popped the chalky tablets. "It's worth the burn."

Her smile lit up the dark room. Some of the

tension eased in his chest. He told himself it was the fast-acting antacids.

"I'm sorry I woke you."

"It wasn't you. Jack was restless." Her eyes went misty soft. "I saw your scar. My father told me you almost lost your arm in the war. Is that what disturbed your sleep? Bad dreams?"

He froze. "I don't talk about that."

"Maybe you should. Maybe it would help you sleep."

"It's over. My arm is fine. No good comes from rehashing old business."

"No good comes from bottling up old wounds. Talking can help."

"I've heard that psychobabble before." He crossed his arms over his chest. "What possible good can come from splitting my veins open and bleeding emotions?"

"Maybe you'd find some peace."

"What do you want to hear? That I cost my best friend his life? Or that I'd give my arm to have him back? What's the cost of a limb compared to the life of a husband and father?"

She blanched but didn't back down. "Life isn't that simple. You were in a war."

"We traded duty. He was shot as I was re-

lieving him. If our positions had been reversed, I'd be the one sent home in a pine
box."

"And if you hadn't changed assignments,
the shooter might have shot to the right or
the left and your friend would still be gone.
You can play the if game all night long, but
it doesn't change anything," she said softly.
"Death happens."

"Quentin's death is on my hands. It's not
something I can be philosophical about."

"I guess not. Try remembering you didn't
kill him."

"Right." He mocked her. "I'll remember
that."

She tried to shrug off his rudeness, but he
saw the cringe she couldn't hide. Why didn't
she just go back to bed?

"So Christy is Quentin's daughter. She and
her mother are what brought you to River
Run?"

"How—" Her knowledge stunned Nate
until he remembered he'd mentioned Christy
their first night together. "They don't concern you."

"Oh." The animation went out of her face.
"Good night then."

He was such a moron. This was his problem. And no business of hers. But he figured she'd only been trying to help. He needed to cut her some slack.

"So Jack was restless?" he said quickly before she could leave and go back to bed.

"Yes." She rubbed her hands over her arms, seeking warmth. "He doesn't like the powdered milk bottles as well as his formula bottles. I think it upsets his stomach a little."

"Speaking of which…" He walked past her, inhaled the sweet scent of lotion that made her skin so silky soft and pulled open the refrigerator, showing her the light.

"We have electricity." She clapped her hands. "That means the storm is over, right?"

"It means the hub is up and working."

"Oh, come on, give me some hope here." She closed the refrigerator door and leaned back against it, putting her way too close. "I'm stir-crazy. I need to see something besides the inside of this house. Even the slim pickings in River Run will do."

"For once we're in agreement." He stepped back and bumped into the counter. She smelled too good, looked too soft, and he found it too easy to remember how sweet she tasted. Being alone with her like this was not good. Not for him. "I appreciate your cooking, but I can really go for some of Luigi's Pizza."

"Oh, my God, Luigi's Pizza! How could I forget Luigi's Pizza? Their pepperoni is to die for. I swear I ate there three times a week my senior year in high school." She sighed over the memory, her breasts rising and falling under the soft fabric of his T-shirt. He forced his eyes back to her face. "You are so on. As soon as the snowplows clear the roads we have a date."

She flounced back to bed, and he scrubbed his hands over his face. That really hadn't gone according to plan.

"Freedom." Michelle flung her arms out wide, embracing the beautiful outdoors. Crisp and clear, the air still held the icy bite of winter but a single ray of sunshine promised the storm truly had ended. "My kingdom for freedom."

And the roads were plowed, including their driveway—one of the perks of living with the sheriff. Nate had taken off at first light promising to be back by early afternoon to take her grocery shopping.

He missed that deadline by several hours. No surprise.

She'd brooded for a while at being under the thumb of another lawman, the pacing and waiting taking her back to too many memories from the past.

Like the time she walked to school through huge drifts of snow one year after a storm knocked out power for three days. The snow had stopped and Dad was gone so she got dressed and trudged to the school four blocks away, only to find out Dad had forgotten to tell her school was canceled for the rest of the week. She was out the next week because of a bad case of bronchitis and missed the field trip to the capitol building in Sacramento.

After a while she shook off the negativity of being out of control. Instead she and Jack went out to the garage and started sanding the rocker. Okay, she sanded and Jack slept in a blanket-draped drawer, the point being they kept busy until Nate showed up.

Now they were off to town for some much-needed supplies.

And much-needed company.

If she had to spend another minute alone with hunky sheriff Nate, she might spontaneously combust. Something about the man kept her body on a low-level buzz.

"Wouldn't that be queendom?" Nate came out of the house carrying Jack in his car seat.

He wasn't immune to her, either. Sometimes she caught him looking at her with such heat she wanted to eliminate the space between them and forget they could barely tolerate being in the same room together.

Oh, yeah, she needed civilization bad.

"Queendom. I like that. But right now I'll settle for River Run."

"I bet that's something you never thought you'd say."

"You got that right." She strapped her seat belt on. "Luigi's, driver, and make it quick."

Nate gave her an askance glance before he put his big SUV in gear and rolled forward.

"You're a little tipsy on your freedom there, aren't you?"

"Yes." She sighed, making no effort to deny

it. "It was getting so I couldn't breathe. It didn't seem to bother you. But then you left at the crack of dawn. You've been free all day."

"I've been working. And I hadn't had a break in close to a month. I was glad to be able to get some things done that I'd been putting off."

"I got some song writing done, too. But I'm still happy to be free." She breathed deeply, let it out slowly. "Did you put an arrest warrant out for Jack's mom?"

"No." His hands fisted on the wheel. "But I listed her as a person of interest, which means information on her will be forwarded to me if she shows up on the grid anywhere we share info."

"What will you do when you find her?"

"I don't know," he admitted, surprising her. "I hate how she abandoned Jack. It's hard for me to get past that. He's probably better off without her."

"Probably?"

"Some women aren't meant to be mothers."

Now that was interesting. Did he speak from personal experience or just from what he'd seen?

"And you feel confident in making that decision for him?"

The look he gave her sliced her to the bone. Which made her wonder why. Why was she pushing? Obviously her question pricked a sore spot for him. But it was none of her business. And sure, Jack was a cute kid, but the last thing she needed was to get emotionally involved in this mess.

"Never mind," she said as if his look hadn't cut her off at the knees. "I'm sure you'll work it all out." Seeing they were still in the driveway, she waved her fingers at him. "Luigi's! Forthwith."

"Freak." He sighed and pulled into the street.

"You have no sense of fun," she informed him.

"I know how to have fun," he stated evenly.

"Jack is the one I feel sorry for. You really should put a little effort in for his sake."

"Don't tell me how to raise Jack."

"I'm just saying the kid deserves a chance."

"Cut it out." He sent her a sideways glare. "I know how to have a good time as much as the next guy."

"Doing what?" she demanded, not believing him for a minute. She'd never met a man that was more work-oriented, except for her father and that wasn't saying much. "What do you do for fun? Play football with the guys? Go fishing? My dad liked to fish. Or are you a secret gamer? Confess, you get your thrills on *Grand Theft Auto*, don't you?"

"What's *Grand Theft Auto*?"

She shook her head in exaggerated disappointment. "Now that's just sad."

"I'm a law enforcement officer. Why would I play something called *Grand Theft Auto*?"

"Oh, I don't know, for the vicarious thrill? Or maybe because *it's fun*?"

Now it was a killer glare. "I don't have to explain myself to you."

"No, you don't." Satisfied she'd riled him, she wiggled more comfortably into her seat. "If you put on the siren so we get to Luigi's extra fast, I'll let you play *Grand Theft Auto* when we get home."

"That's not going to happen."

"It would in my queendom."

He shook his head, but she saw the corner of his mouth quirk up. A smile. They rode in silence for several blocks.

"I work out. And I like to bowl," he finally muttered.

Pleased with herself, she drew an exclamation point in the condensation on the window.

CHAPTER SIX

LUIGI'S was packed. Seemed everyone had a case of cabin fever and decided to eat out tonight. Nate bounced Jack and scanned the room looking for Kim and Christy.

The kid weighed next to nothing. Nate could hold him in one hand. Not that he would. He still worried he might break the little guy.

It was hard to remember Christy was ever this small. He'd thought he was being a help to Kim in those early days. And he probably was, but he knew now she'd needed so much more than he'd given her.

He'd gone ahead with his plan to call her and asked her to meet him here tonight. With Michelle along it wasn't quite what he'd had in mind, but it was a start. And with Kim there nobody was likely to get the wrong idea about him and Michelle. Especially Michelle.

He spotted Kim talking to her neighbor David, an average-size man with dark hair and a trim mustache. She laughed at something he said, and then she caught sight of Nate and waved. The man picked up Christy and the small group started making its way through the restaurant toward him.

"Looks like your friend has company," Michelle observed. "Maybe we should look for a bigger booth."

He turned and found her tucking a high chair in at the end of a booth. "That won't be necessary. David won't be joining us."

"I'm betting he will," she contradicted him, her gaze on the group about to join them. "I hope you don't have any feelings in that direction."

"What do you mean?" he demanded. "Why do you say that?"

"Because it looks to me like the widow is smitten with David."

"You're wrong." He dismissed her claim. Kim still loved Quentin. Nate would know if that had changed. Quentin may be gone but his spirit was irreplaceable.

"Hi, Nate." Kim greeted him with a big hug. "This was a great idea. You know David, right? It's such a crush in here. You don't mind if he joins us, do you?"

Michelle jumped in. "Of course not. Hi, I'm Michelle Ross."

"Sheriff Ross's daughter." Kim patted Michelle's shoulder in unspoken sympathy. "I'm Kim and this is my daughter, Christy. She's three, and she'll talk your ear off if you let her."

"Michelle." David greeted Michelle with a fond smile. "It's good to see you. May I say how sorry I am about your father's passing? The whole town misses him. I would have been at the services, but I covered the office so my father could go."

"Thank you." Michelle graciously offered her hand and Dave swallowed it up in his large mitts. She didn't seem to notice as she continued. "Those two did like to cast a line together. I was always happy when your dad was free on Saturday mornings. It meant I got some extra beauty sleep."

Nate scowled at the chitchat. He didn't care for the way David hung on to Michelle's hand. The man needed to move on. Didn't he see they were blocking traffic standing around the table?

He made a point of scanning the area. "Sorry, buddy," he told David, "but it doesn't look like any of the bigger booths are available."

"Don't be ridiculous, Nate." Kim waved him off. "We can squeeze in here." She slid onto the bench seat and pulled David in beside her. "Here, there's room in the window for the baby seat." She lowered the handle and shoved the seat on the window ledge.

Unhappy with the way things were shaking out, Nate glanced at Michelle. She winked and scooted in to sit across from Kim. He narrowed his eyes at her, but she just smiled and released Jack from his seat.

"I see you finally got that peach-fuzz mustache to grow in properly," she teased David.

"Brat." He grinned and swiped fingers over the hair framing his upper lip.

"He had such a baby face when he first joined his dad's dental practice, the older ladies gave him a bad time. So he decided to grow a mustache to look older."

"It worked, too." He shook a finger at Michelle. "And it was never as bad as you make out."

"Of course not." She looked at Kim and mouthed, "Peach fuzz."

Kim laughed. She inspected David. "I like it."

Nate shifted in his seat, feeling like an outsider. Thankfully, the waitress arrived to take their order. After a brief consult he ordered one vegetarian and one meat-lover's pizza.

"Mommy, can I have my juice?" Christy asked.

Kim pulled a sippy cup from her purse and David passed it to the little girl.

Once she had her drink, Christy patted Nate's hand and pointed at Jack. "Baby."

"That's right." He bopped her nose with a finger. "That's Jack."

"He sure is a cutie," Kim told Michelle. "How old is he?"

"Around four months."

"I didn't know you had a son," David said. "I'm surprised your dad wasn't crowing about his grandson every chance he got."

"Oh, no." Michelle shook her head, her gold hair brushing over her shoulders. She cocked her thumb in his direction. "He's Nate's."

Clearly shocked, Kim's gaze ricocheted

around as if she didn't know where to look. She finally took refuge in snagging David's gaze.

Nate realized he should have taken charge of the introductions. Found a time to make an explanation to Kim when they didn't have an audience. He wanted her help, but he didn't want to put his life on display for strangers.

"Ah, Nate," Michelle whispered.

Used to hiding his emotions, he flicked an expressionless glare at David, wishing him away. He'd prefer Michelle wasn't there, either, and not just because she kept digging her elbow into his ribs.

"Kim, I can explain," he began.

"Nate, you don't have to—"

"I want to. We've been friends for years—"

"Nate—" Michelle suddenly shoved at him "—I really need to talk to you."

He turned his head and looked down at her. "Not now." He focused on Kim. "Jack was a surprise."

"Please, you two, don't argue," Kim implored. "This is a special time for you."

"Kim, it's not what you think," Michelle countered.

Again Kim's gaze went to David, and Nate

thought she was wishing for some privacy. He echoed that sentiment. He knew he was handling this badly. He should have planned out what he was going to say, but he'd been distracted by Michelle. And Jack, of course.

"Kim, I was really hoping—"

Michelle stopped him by turning his head toward her, and grinding her mouth on his.

For a moment his mind went blank. And his body took over, responding to the sweet softness of her lips under his. He opened his mouth, tasting her, devouring, her before his brain reengaged.

Furious, he grabbed her hand and pulled her from the booth.

Michelle let Nate drag her away from the table, stopping only long enough to hand Jack over to Kim with a grateful smile.

He kept hold of her hand until they reached the video games at the back of the room near the restrooms.

"Are you insane?" he demanded. "I'm trying to explain the situation to Kim. I have a personal interest in making sure she fully understands what's going on."

"I know." She tugged at the hem of her waist-length sweater. "You're welcome."

"That settles it. You are nuts."

"No, I'm saving you from yourself. I get it, okay. I know your grand plan was to get together with the widow and raise your kids together." She was pretty good at reading people—as a songwriter she observed life— and interpersonal relationships. Plus, the man was as transparent as cellophane.

"You couldn't be more wrong. Her husband was my best friend. She's like a sister to me." His affront couldn't be more obvious, and she realized she'd misread the situation. His ire showed in his stance. "You have no right interfering in my personal affairs. Or giving Kim the impression that something is going on between us."

"Me? The way you bumbled that explanation, the woman thinks I had your baby!"

"No."

"Yes. Look, I know you think you need to play hero because you feel responsible for Kim being a widow—"

"You don't know anything about me, or my intentions. The last thing I am is a hero."

"Whatever. This is what I see, you're fixated on the past and she's ready to move on."

"What? Who with—David?" He scoffed. "Now you're being ridiculous. Kim still loves Quentin."

She sighed. Men could be so dense. "She'll always love Quentin but she's also a young vital woman with a full life ahead of her. She's found a new love. She and David are a couple. You're going to have to deal."

"You don't know what you're talking about." He dismissed her claim. "How could you? You haven't spoken to anyone in town for seven months."

"How can you be a law enforcement officer and not see what's in front of your eyes?"

"Maybe because there's nothing to see."

Aggravated by his failure to listen to her, she grabbed his broad shoulders and tried to turn him toward the table they'd just left.

He didn't budge.

With a sigh she walked around him, forcing him to turn to keep track of her or stand facing the back wall.

When he faced her, she waved her hand, inviting him to take in the couple cooing at the baby. As they watched, Kim lifted her face to David's for a kiss. Ouch.

Michelle rolled her gaze up to Nate. He stood, hands on hips, his eyes locked on the wife of his best friend embracing another man. His expression never changed as the seconds ticked by and she wondered what he was thinking.

Deciding she'd give him a moment alone, she patted his arm and headed back to the booth. She went two steps before his arm wrapped around her waist and he swept her into his arms.

"Hey…" She pushed against his chest.

"Just saying thanks." He bent his head to hers and claimed her mouth. Slanting his head, he deepened the kiss with a sweep of his tongue. No hesitation, no holding back, no distractions, this kiss was unlike any others they'd shared. He held her with care, with urgency. He tasted good and felt better.

The pizza parlor disappeared as she melted against him, and his heat surrounded her. The buzz she constantly fought to ignore ignited into full-blown tingles. Desire flowed hot through her blood as she opened to his sensual demand.

Needing to get closer she went onto her tiptoes and circled his neck with her arms. And suddenly she felt like she floated on air, Nate her only anchor in a swirling mist of sensation.

Someone jostled her from behind.

"Excuse me," a young voice said, followed by teenaged giggles.

"Sheriff Nate has a girl."

The shrill announcement echoed through Michelle's head, disrupting her passionate haze.

"That kiss was hot," a girlish voice replied in awe.

Michelle's eyes popped open and she stared into Nate's heated gaze. A breath shuddered through his wide chest, her body moving along with his. That's when she realized the floating sensation came from the fact he held her aloft.

"You..." She cleared her throat. "You should put me down."

He leaned over and her feet gently settled on the ground. For a moment his hands lingered on her waist and then he released her.

She brushed the back of her fingers down his cheek. "Well done."

"What?" She took satisfaction in hearing the rasp of desire in the word.

"You used me. And I don't even care."

"You started it."

She held up a hand. "Don't push it. Your pride needed a booster shot and I was handy. I get it. Don't do it again."

Facing the room, she tugged at the hem of her purple sweater and willed her overheated body to settle down.

"You know you have to correct the impression Jack is our child."

"Nobody would believe that."

She shook her head at his obtuseness. "You'll see."

"Come on." A hand in the small of her back ushered her forward.

The man really had no clue. They'd gone half a dozen steps when a couple stopped them to congratulate them on their little bundle of joy. Michelle flicked him a telling glance, smiled at the couple and moved on to their booth.

She scooted in, slid a piece of meat-lover's pizza onto her plate and took a big bite. Jack slept against Kim's shoulder. Michelle eyed the hands clasped together on the table and felt a smidgen of sympathy for Nate.

A moment later he slid in beside her and reached for his own slice. In a disconnected part of her brain she noticed that both of them had taken the meat pie while Kim and David had both chosen the veggie.

"Please tell them the truth," she prompted him.

He shrugged. "It's my business."

"And my reputation," she countered.

"You're leaving town, what do you care?"

"I care." She faced the couple avidly drinking in their debate. "Kim, Jack isn't my child. He's Nate's cousin's boy."

"Oh." Kim looked confused. "I thought Jack passed away a few months ago."

"Yes, and his girlfriend was pregnant. She left the baby on Nate's porch the first night of the storm."

"Oh, my God," Kim exclaimed. She softly rubbed the sleeping baby's back. "His mother left him in the storm? He could have died."

"Luckily, I heard him crying."

Kim glanced back and forth between Michelle and Nate, her expression a curious combination of understanding and skepticism.

"Why didn't you just say so?" Kim asked Nate. His cheeks turned ruddy. "This didn't seem the place to go into it. I'm not used to discussing my business in such an open forum."

Kim's gaze shifted to Michelle, pinning her to her seat. "And where do you fit into the picture?"

"I was at the house when Nate found the baby. We've been stuck together for three days."

"Because she broke into my house."

"My house," she corrected through clenched teeth. "And that's what you choose to share?"

Smug, he lifted one shoulder, let it drop.

Aggrieved all over again. Michelle turned to David. "Who is this gal Dad was shacked up with? I didn't know he'd moved out of the house."

"Ah." David blinked in surprise at suddenly being in the hot seat of the volatile conversation. "You know, he and Dolly had been friends for years. That mild heart attack he had just before his birthday last year scared him. Shortly after your visit he moved in with her."

Silence followed the explanation. Dad and Dolly...lovers? Michelle would never have guessed. Then again, she tended to shy away from any notion of Dad and a lover in the same thought.

"More pizza, please." Christy's small voice piped into the stillness. Kim reached for a veggie slice, but the little girl spoke up. "No, Mommy, I want pepperoni."

"Here you go, sweet thing." Nate placed a small slice on her plate.

"Thank you, Uncle Nate." She smiled, grabbed a round bite of pepperoni and popped it in her mouth.

Kim reached over and patted Nate's hand. "Jack couldn't be in better hands."

"Yet, I'm already making mistakes."

Annoyed as she was at his closemouthed attitude, Michelle felt a little sorry for him. Tonight was definitely not going as he'd planned. Time for a change of mood.

"You'll fix it," she stated confidently. "You better—" she smiled at him, showing a lot of teeth "—or I'll sue you for child support."

Next to her Nate went very still, and then he threw back his head and laughed out loud. He pushed a fall of hair behind her ear.

"You'd probably get it, too."

"Oh, believe it. Judge Austin is my god-father."

Still chuckling, he groaned. "Of course he is."

"You know, Nate, I have Christy's baby furniture stored in the garage. You're welcome to use it for Jack. There's a crib, and a changing table. Plus I think I still have her baby swing."

"Kim, that would be great. I don't know what to say."

"Thank you?"

"Of course. Thank you. I'll pick it up tomorrow."

"I have a truck," David said. "You must be really busy with the aftermath of the storm. Why don't I pack it up and bring it over? Then, if you're not available, I can help set it up."

Nate nodded and expressed his thanks. He managed to sound sincere even though Michelle knew deep down he was totally frustrated.

His phone beeped. He pulled it from his pocket and checked the screen. "I have to take this," he said and slid from the booth to step into the lobby.

"Mommy, can I ride the pony?" Christy pointed at a shiny brown pony with a red saddle.

"I'll take her," David volunteered and lifted

the girl into his arms. They wandered off toward the pony.

"Here." Michelle reached for Jack's carrier. "Let's put him in his seat. Your poor arm is probably ready to fall off." She stood, gently took the baby and tucked him into place.

"You're good for him," Kim observed.

"Jack? He's a sweetheart."

"I meant Nate."

"Ha." Michelle made no effort to hide her derision. "We're lucky we didn't kill each other during the storm."

"Hmm. Like that killer kiss?"

"Please. He was punishing me because I was right."

Kim lifted one fine eyebrow. "And it hurt so good?"

Michelle grinned and fanned herself. "I didn't say I didn't like it."

"I've never seen him laugh like that. We're usually lucky to get a few chuckles out of him."

Michelle set Jack's carrier on the bench seat and sat down next to him, her attention wandering to Nate, who stood staring intently out the front window while he dealt with his call.

"Yeah, well, he's not a lighthearted guy."

"No, he's not," Kim agreed with a sigh. "And that's what I love about David."

"Nate seemed a little surprised by David." Michelle liked Kim; she was smart, perceptive and not threatened by Michelle, which sometimes women were. "I think he's put you on a pedestal."

"Which is why I haven't mentioned David." She met Michelle square in the eye. "I think you saved us both from an embarrassing moment."

Michelle simply stared back. Kim sighed. "I love Nate like a brother. He was a lifesaver after Quentin died. But I'm not a stone statue. I deserve true love. I had it once and I won't settle for less this time. Nate is one of the best men I know. But he doesn't understand because a strong relationship is not something he's ever known. I want it for him. He deserves to be loved. He deserves someone who can make him laugh out loud."

CHAPTER SEVEN

STILL half-asleep Michelle pushed open the bathroom door and stepped inside. She promptly bumped into a steam-slicked body.

Instantly alert she stepped back and ogled Nate in nothing but a towel. His shoulders looked impossibly wide over a broad chest and a rippling six-pack.

The man was fine. And better than a cup of Joe first thing in the morning.

"Mmm. Good morning."

She got a growl in response.

Too bad he was a bad-tempered Neanderthal.

She reached for her toothbrush and took a peek at her own reflection. Her hair was a wild explosion of curls and her face devoid of makeup, but she wore her midnight-blue shorty pajamas. Not too bad a showing first thing in the morning.

"The room is taken," he said around his own toothbrush.

"I don't mind sharing," she assured him.

"I do," he barked.

She ignored him, enjoying instead the play of muscles in his arm and abdomen as he cleaned his teeth.

"Why aren't you using the master suite?" she asked him. "You could have a bathroom all to yourself there."

"I was already settled in my room when your dad decided to move out. I had the house to myself so I saw no reason to move. You take it."

"I'm good in my old room. I won't be here long enough to need the bigger room."

"Thank God."

"Hey, I'm helping you out here," she reminded him. "Have you thought what you're going to do now your girlfriend has found someone new?"

"Not funny. I need to talk to Kim," he declared as he rinsed his brush and returned it to the medicine cabinet, which was meticulously in order. "This thing with David may not be serious."

She rolled her eyes, amazed at his ability

for self-deception. "She was kissing him in public."

"We were kissing in public. There's nothing serious between us."

He had her there. And if his easy dismissal of their embrace stung a little, she pretended not to notice.

"It looked serious to me."

"That's not what I need to talk to her about. I want to discuss Jack's care. She'll be able to help me explore my options."

She relaxed and nodded. "Closure is a good thing."

"Ouch!" He pulled his razor away from a bleeding nick. "There's no need for anything girly like closure." He glared at her reflection in the mirror. "Can I have some privacy, please?"

Sighing, she tugged at the hem of her pajama top and for a moment it molded to the naked breasts beneath the thin cloth. His gaze lowered and his jaw clenched.

Satisfied, she turned on her heel.

"Seems to me you're the one acting like a girl," she ventured. "Next time lock the door if you're so modest."

A curse sounded from the other side of the closed door.

She smirked, suddenly looking forward to the day.

Twenty minutes later she shuffled down the stairs, Jack in her arms, to find Nate walking out the front door.

"Hey." She stopped him. "We need to make plans for shopping. The cupboards are bare and Jack has needs."

He turned to face her, a scowl drawing his dark brows together. He rubbed his temple as his gaze glazed over and his thoughts focused inward.

They'd planned to do some grocery shopping after dinner last night, but it turned out he needed to go back to the office. Instead they swung by the market and he ran in to pick up some formula and diapers. She'd almost kissed him again when she also found coffee and milk in the bag.

But kissing the man was getting to be a habit she needed to break. Seriously, did she have no sense of self-preservation?

He came toward her almost as if he'd read her mind and meant to test her resolve. It took everything in her to hold her ground.

He stopped next to her and bent to kiss Jack on the top of his head.

"We're not going to get everything we need here in River Run. We need to drive down to Sacramento to hit one of the big warehouse stores and a Wal-Mart."

Her heart sung at that decree. "Excellent idea."

"I'll work it out so I leave early. Can you be ready at three?"

"You bet. Jack and I'll be here with our shopping shoes on."

"Uncle Nate is going to be late," Michelle informed Jack after getting off the phone with Nate. He was a cop. Of course he was going to be late. "Get used to it."

She used the extra time to wander out into the backyard. She already had a list of supplies for work on the rocking chair, and changes she'd decided on for updating the kitchen, master suite and downstairs bathroom.

She intended to do the inside work herself; the outside work, not so much. Gardening had been her dad's thing, not hers. The yard work she'd hire out. But she spied the tree house and her heart melted.

That was something her dad had really done right.

Some of her happiest memories were the two years she went to Princess Camp and the hours spent in her castle tree house. The castle started out painted lavender, but in her teen years she toned the color down to a soft gray. By the weathered look of it her dad hadn't done anything with it since she moved away. She mentally added lavender paint to her list.

And a note to call Elle and Amanda. Thoughts of Princess Camp reminded her she hadn't spoken to her longtime friends since before she arrived in River Run.

Her cell rang and she fished her phone from her jeans pocket. Speak of the princesses.

"Elle, I was just thinking about you and Amanda."

"Really? Am I supposed to be telepathic to communicate now? What's wrong with the phone? See I picked up my cell, punched a number and there you were on the other end."

"Witch. Don't pick on me. I'm stuck in the middle of nowhere and until yesterday a storm had knocked out electricity and phone services. It's downright primitive."

"A storm knocked out services for three days?"

"Technically two days, but spring is a day away and we have snow on the ground. You live in San Diego. You wouldn't understand."

"Hmm. You have me there. So how long are you planning to stay in the back of beyond? I'm anxious to see you."

"Bad news. It's going to be longer than I thought. Turns out my dad rented his house to the new sheriff. His lease isn't up for a few months."

"So you can't work on the house?" Elle demanded, eagerness adding a lilt to the question. "Come stay with me, we can scope out L.A. on weekends and find you a place while you're waiting for the tenant to vacate the house."

Everything in Michelle leaped at the suggestion, but she'd given her word to help Nate with Jack. And with Jack's light weight resting trustingly against her shoulder, she couldn't discount her promise.

"I can't."

"What? Why not? If you're thinking of the rent, don't. I have it covered."

"You are the greatest. But you have to stop tempting me, because I have to stay. I made a commitment."

"You hate that place."

"I know. It's complicated."

"Ah." A knowing quality entered Elle's voice. "There's a man involved."

A vision of Nate half-naked in the bathroom this morning streamed through her mind. She sighed and kissed Jack's downy-soft hair.

"Two actually."

"Hmm." Elle hummed knowingly. "That would be complicated. Promise me it's not going to keep you from moving south."

"Not a chance."

"Good. Listen, I have a meeting. Keep in touch, and I don't mean telepathically."

"Very funny. Can you tell what I'm thinking now?"

She laughed. "There's the Michelle I know and love. Tootles."

Michelle disconnected, a grin lifting her mood. She missed her friends.

The time on the phone caught her attention. Nate should be here soon. She moved inside to finish getting ready. In case he arrived on time she wanted to be waiting when he got there.

Too late. Apparently he was early, which was almost as bad as being late.

He came skipping down the stairs as she entered the front hall. He must have been faster than he'd thought because he'd obviously showered and changed.

He wore black slacks and a long-sleeved, light blue shirt with a navy pin-striped tie and carried a black blazer.

She whistled her appreciation. "Don't you look pretty? Do you always dress so formal to go shopping?"

"I have an appointment with an attorney about assuming custody of Jack," Nate said, hooking his jacket over the end of the banister. "I had to put the mayor off and hurry home because the attorney couldn't adjust the appointment without moving it back two weeks. Child Protective Services needs a copy of the petition. So I'm going to have to drop you at the warehouse store and catch up with you after the meeting."

"Of course you have to make the appointment." She indicated her sweater and jeans. "It'll just take me a minute to change."

"There's no need. And we're already running late."

"I can't go like this. I'll be quick." She thrust Jack into Nate's arms and waved to the baby's gear. "I'll be there before you get Jack loaded up and strapped in." She dashed up the stairs.

Knowing she'd never live it down if she didn't meet her promised speed limit, she kicked her shoes off on the way to the closet, pulled out black pumps and a short black skirt. It took two minutes to shimmy out of her jeans and into the skirt. She looked into the mirror and nodded—the light pink sweater was fine. She clicked a wide black belt around her waist and ran out the door.

At the bottom of the stairs she slipped into the pumps, grabbed her purse and the jacket she noticed Nate had left hanging over the banister and strolled out to the SUV.

Nate was just closing the garage door as she walked up. The once-over he gave her was gratifying. The obvious male approval stroked her ego. But when he opened his mouth she knew it wouldn't be to compliment her shoes.

"You forgot your jacket," she said and thrust the black garment into his hands. And then she made a point of reaching her seat before he slid into his.

While strapping in she glanced behind her to make sure Jack was properly situated and noticed he sat in a new seat. He was scoring big today. Along with the furniture they dropped off earlier Kim had brought a bag of clothes Christy had outgrown. Gender neutral, of course.

He wore a pair of brown jeans with a pale yellow shirt with a bee buzzing along the front. Under it he wore a white onesie and on top should be a bib that read Got Formula.

"What happened to Jack's bib?" she asked Nate as they hit the road.

"I threw it away."

"What? Why?"

"It was purple."

"It was white."

"With purple writing. He's a boy, he's not going to wear purple."

"He can't read, doesn't know the difference between purple and polka dots and—pay attention here because this is really important—he's only four months old."

"Which only means I have to protect his manhood until he can do it himself."

"And purple lettering is over the line?"

"Yes."

She shook her head at his unrelenting masculine stance. No wonder men and women didn't understand each other. They were taught from birth to be contrary.

"What time is your appointment?" she asked, changing the subject.

"Four-thirty."

She glanced at her watch—three-twenty. Sacramento was a good hour and a half from River Run.

"Will he wait if you're late?"

"He said he'd wait as long as he could."

"You'd better go straight there." She stated the obvious. "Jack's future is more important than a few supplies. How did you choose this lawyer?"

"Dolly recommended him."

Dolly, retired attorney and Dad's girlfriend. Michelle knew she'd have to go see the woman, but she dreaded the thought. She really didn't want to talk about her dad's relationship or their mutual loss.

He turned right onto the on ramp to Highway 80 and then glanced her way. "You're sure you don't mind waiting?"

"Not when it's best for Jack."

"Best? I'm a sheriff," he said, facing forward again. "I heard you warning him against the perils of living with a lawman."

"There's that, but you've been very good with him, patient and caring. And at least you're trying, which is more than can be said for the woman who dropped him off."

"I thought you were giving her the benefit of the doubt."

"I never said that. I said she may have knocked and we didn't hear her. That didn't mean it was acceptable for her to leave him in the freezing cold."

"I'm glad to hear it." He loosened the tie around his neck.

Michelle meant what she said. And she meant to leave it at that but she couldn't.

"I know she doesn't deserve a second chance. That there's no excuse for leaving her baby in a dangerous situation. I get that, I really do. But there's this tiny part of me that keeps saying I'd have done anything to know my mom."

Silence met her revelation, leaving her feeling exposed. She glanced at Nate's hard profile, found no hint of his thoughts and turned her gaze to the tree-rich scene out her window.

"I guess it's not something you can understand if you grew up with your mom."

There was a sigh beside her. "My mom should never have had a child. She had the maturity of a fifteen-year-old. Which is a personal assessment, not a professional one. Everything was always about her. And if it was too hard, or took too long, she didn't want to be bothered."

"Sounds rough." She'd longed for some freedom, a little less supervision, but it seemed you could have too much of a good thing.

"It wasn't bad when my dad was alive. He loved taking care of her. He was proud of his home and his family. He took care of everything. She cooked. She had a weekly menu that she repeated week after week."

Okay, that part didn't sound so bad. The

Lord knew her dad hadn't been very imaginative in the kitchen.

"And then Dad died."

She flinched. That was bad. "How old were you?"

"Six."

"That's pretty young."

"She could barely function after my dad died. Everything fell to me. I had to get us up for work and school. I had to remind her to shop for food and to pay the bills. I kept expecting her to become the mom, but she never did. She loved me but my needs were always second to hers. I don't want that for Jack."

Of course he wouldn't. His mother had robbed him of a childhood. Michelle understood where he was coming from, but that little voice continued to call to her.

"But you loved her, too."

His shoulders tensed and for a moment she didn't think he'd respond.

"Yeah." It was grudgingly offered.

"Do you think your life would have been better without her?" she wondered aloud.

"It's hard to say," he answered, unsure. "Foster care is no picnic. But there are good people in the system, as well."

"So you're sure this is what you want to do? You want full custody?"

"I owe it to Jack, to my Uncle Stan."

And that wasn't a hard choice to contemplate. The silence grew between them until finally she had to ask.

"Have you heard anything on his mother's whereabouts?"

He slid Michelle a sideways glance. "You're like a dog with a bone, aren't you?"

"That must mean yes." She grinned. "What have you learned?"

"Not much. She and Jack lived in Carson City. Searching across states complicates things, but I'll find her."

"And then?"

He lifted one shoulder, let it drop. "I don't know. The letter made it clear she was done with Jack. She wanted me to assume custody. Or give him to a good home. She couldn't be any clearer in her intentions. Finding her probably won't change anything."

"But you don't know that."

"I know Jack's future is too important to base it on maybes and what-ifs. And the attorney made it clear on the phone if I wait to assume custody, Child Services may step in."

* * *

Traffic was light so Nate pulled up to the attorney's office only ten minutes late. It helped that Michelle had agreed to wait.

She surprised him sometimes. She wore her siren facade so well that when she showed signs of depth it caught him off guard. Heaven help him, but he'd told her more about himself than anyone else, ever.

Why was that? What was there about her that made him open up?

She wondered why he had so little sympathy for Jack's mom; he could tell her he knew how it felt to be left in a storm.

He'd been a latchkey kid. They'd lived only a block from the school so he walked, and one day when he was in the first grade he'd run home through the rain only to huddle wet and cold on the doorstep for over an hour waiting for her to get home.

As he'd told Michelle, he firmly believed some women weren't meant to be mothers.

He stepped out of the vehicle and grabbed his jacket. When he saw no movement from her, he bent down to ask, "Aren't you going to come in and wait in the lobby?"

She shook her head, causing her hair to shimmer like gold in the dying sunshine.

"Jack is asleep. We'll wait here. Take as long as you need."

He nodded and turned to enter the modern glass building. The entrance faced the small parking lot and Ted Watkins was waiting at the door.

They shook hands and he gestured to the SUV where he could clearly see Michelle.

"Would your friend like to come in? We have a nice waiting room."

"Thank you. But the baby is asleep."

"You have Jack with you?" Ted's gaze went back to the SUV. "Good. I'd like to meet him."

"Why?" Nate's protective hackles rose.

"Because it makes it more personal when I see and talk to the people involved in a case. Child custody cases are extremely personal so I want that connection. I'd also like to document his condition, take some pictures for the file."

"For what reason?" This really wasn't going how Nate had expected. "The trauma he experienced from being left in the storm has passed."

He spread his hands. "It may not ever come into play, but I prefer to be prepared. And as an officer of the court I can add my evaluation along with the custody documentation."

Watkins cocked his head and met Nate stare for stare.

"Is there a reason you don't want me to meet the boy?" the attorney asked point-blank.

"No." Nate relaxed a little. He got the impression Ted Watkins wouldn't relent until he determined for himself that Jack was okay. Nate knew his size and air of command intimidated most people. The fact that Watkins didn't let that deter him told Nate everything he needed to know. The man was tough, not afraid of a fight.

He was in the right hands.

"Good, then shall we ask your friend and Jack to join us?"

CHAPTER EIGHT

"I saw the baby furniture in the room across the hall. I guess David delivered everything."

"He did." Keeping her attention on the array of stains and paint on the shelf, Michelle smiled at Nate's terse tone. "Between the three of us we got it all upstairs and put together. I like Kim. And David. They seem really happy together."

"You already made your point there," he said grimly. "We're not going to talk about their relationship."

"Okay, fine. What did the attorney say?" After being introduced to the lawyer, she and Jack had waited in the reception area while Nate finished his business.

"Can't we talk about the weather?"

Concerned, she stopped and faced him. "It was that bad?"

"No." His expression softened and he

cupped the side of her face in his large hand. Briefly, gently, he swept his thumb along her cheek before dropping his hand.

"I liked him. He doesn't anticipate any problem with the court granting me full custody."

"Good." She forced a smile, pretending she didn't already miss his touch. He was an uptight lawman, in a go-nowhere town, and he stood between her and what she needed to do to get out of said nowhere town. Yet a single caress melted her insides.

That was just wrong.

Intent on self-preservation, she turned back to the shelves. They'd already been to the warehouse store to pick up food and baby supplies. They were now at Wal-Mart and had half the baby section loaded into two carts. Jack sat propped up between her oversize purse and a Spider-Man fleece blanket Nate insisted he needed.

Her last chore was to gather the items on her home improvement list. Best to stay on task.

"Whoa." Nate's hand closed around the tin of lavender paint Michelle moved toward her cart. "I said no purple."

"It's not purple. It's lavender."

"Which is just froufrou for purple." He put it back on the shelf. "It's not going in Jack's room."

Michelle tried to reach around him to retrieve the can of paint, but he blocked the shelves with his big body. Hands crossed over his chest, he sidestepped every time she did.

"It's not for Jack's room," she assured him, feinting one way then quickly back the other hoping to catch him off guard. He simply wrapped one long arm around her waist and reeled her in.

"I don't want it anywhere in the house," he declared.

Suddenly breathless and way too close to his taut, muscular body she went still, ending their crazy dance for power.

"Enough." She planted both hands on her hips. "It's not for the house, either. It's for outside."

"You want to paint my house purple? Oh, hell no."

That got her back up. "My house," she corrected. "I'll paint it any color I choose."

"Not while I'm living there," he responded.

"New rule, I get veto power over all improvement projects."

"I don't think so. You haven't put a single bit of yourself in the house. And for the baby's room your idea of decorating is a stuffed bear, a dump truck and a Spider-Man blanket."

"It's a really cool truck."

She threw up her hands. "He's four months old!"

"He's a boy. And he's not going to live in a purple house."

"I give up." She sighed. "The paint is for my castle."

He blinked at her. "What?"

"My castle in the backyard." He still looked blank so she laid it out for him. "Castle. In the tree. In the backyard."

"The tree house?" Comprehension dawned. "That eyesore? I've been waiting for a free day to tear that thing down. It would already be gone by now except for the storm."

Anxiety ripped through her. She was lucky she'd made it home in time to save her beloved haven.

"Is the structure even sound? It's probably ready to fall to the ground."

"It's sound. I had to add a couple of nails here and there but it felt sturdy when I climbed up there yesterday."

"Good Lord." Clearly appalled, he demanded, "Tell me you didn't take Jack up there."

"Oh, yeah, we're a team. I had him in the sling while I was swinging the hammer." Sarcasm screamed through her chipper tone.

"Well, who knows about someone who'd paint any type of house purple?" But he stepped aside and let her retrieve the lavender paint.

An overwhelming sense of sadness hit her as she set the can in the cart. It had nothing to do with the stupid argument—the silly dance had almost been fun. But hearing how close she'd come to losing the tree house made her realize she'd soon be walking away from all of it—the house, the yard, the town. Reality brought on a melancholy she couldn't hide as tears burned her eyes.

"Hey," Nate said softly. He stepped closer, patted her shoulder. "Are you okay? Come on, this can't be about the color of the house."

She shook her head. "It's not that."

"Then what is it?"

His hand fell to the small of her back, a

comforting touch. Without thought she leaned into him about to confess her unexpected wave of nostalgia.

Good God. She stopped, straightened away from him, then carefully put the length of the cart between them.

What was she thinking? She knew better than to reveal her weaknesses. Especially to a lawman trained to spot and exploit the weaknesses of his adversaries.

And despite their close circumstances, they were adversaries.

"It's nothing." She dismissed his concern with a dab at the corner of her eye. "I got a speck of dust in my eye."

"Dust?" He lifted one dark brow.

"Yes." That was it. No more letting her affection for Jack soften her toward his uncle. Surely that's all it was, a little residual connection. "I'm starved. Didn't you promise me dinner? Italian sounds good."

It simply wasn't possible she was falling for the sheriff.

Jack's cries reached Michelle in stereo through the barely open door and the baby monitor on her nightstand. She peeled one eye open, sighed and then forced the other open and her body into motion.

The first move had her moaning as muscles rarely used screamed in discomfort. With the near loss of her beloved tree house fresh in her mind, she went right to work on the remaining repairs and repainting. Nate may consider it a waste of time, stating the new owners could simply tear it down, but it was important to Michelle to bring it to its original glory. It represented the best part of her childhood, a visual reminder her dad had cared for her.

With the help of an electric sander she spent the day getting it ready for its pretty dressing of lavender paint. But tonight her arms and shoulders were feeling the pain of her gain.

No time to stretch with Jack demanding attention from across the hall, but she'd peek in Nate's medicine cabinet for some muscle rub before she went back to bed.

She frowned when the cries suddenly stopped. Not a good sign. A good baby, Jack rarely cried except for his 2:00 a.m. feeding. He'd already figured out if he didn't make himself heard there would be no bottle, and so he announced himself—loudly—until he saw the whites of her eyes.

At least that had been their schedule for the past four nights.

She pushed the door all the way open and found the reason for the change in routine. Nate stood with the baby cradled against his bare chest, Jack's head resting on Nate's shoulder as he rocked him slowly back and forth.

The sight of man and baby together took Michelle's breath away. Her heart wrenched and she wondered what it was about a tough man holding a baby that made a woman's knees go weak? A psychologist would probably explain it as something primal, dealing with procreation and survival of the species.

Whatever. She felt primal all right, lust at its purest level.

Dressed only in lightweight knit pajama bottoms, he personified masculine perfection—broad shoulders, trim torso, taut butt. Muscles flexed and flowed with the controlled back-and-forth motion.

Just yum.

He was gorgeous. Not even the scar detracted from the sheer beauty of his form.

"Hey," he said, sleep giving him a sexy rumble.

She shifted restlessly, and the satin of her nightie brushed over her sensitive nipples. She shivered even as heat raced through her blood.

"Hey." She crossed her arms over her chest, because her body had ideas she had more sense than to give in to. "Nothing wrong with this boy's lungs."

He laughed. "No. What are you doing up?"

"We agreed I'd watch the kid."

"Sure. During the day. I figured we'd split night duty. You had last night. Tonight is my turn."

"Seriously?"

"Yeah." Jack whimpered and began to wiggle, showing his displeasure with the chit-chat delaying his feeding. "But since you're up, can you take him while I get his bottle?"

She took Jack and sung to him softly while Nate disappeared. A few minutes later she heard a ding too close to be from the kitchen downstairs. Curious, she stepped into the hall and encountered Nate coming back from the fourth bedroom, which he'd converted into his office.

He was shaking a bottle he'd obviously just made.

"Are you cheating?" she demanded.

He grinned. "Did I forget to tell you I have a minifridge and microwave in my office?"

"You didn't." She would have noticed when she prowled through the house.

"Okay, I bought them off one of my deputies, who was moving in with his girlfriend. It seemed like a good idea."

"Hmm." She accepted the bottle, fed it to Jack and moved back into the baby's room and the office chair Nate had brought into the room.

He continued to surprise her with his dedication to the whole father thing. "Is it really so easy for you to assume this role?"

He shrugged, a sensual roll of bone and muscle. "Hell no. But it was my choice, no point in moaning about it."

"No, but it's got to be an adjustment."

"You have no idea." He ran both hands through his hair, sending the sleep-tousled mass into further disarray. "Everything has changed. I have to factor him in to every decision I make. Even at work I'm aware there's someone counting on me at home."

"I know," she empathized. "He's young enough and good enough I can put him in the portable crib while I'm working, but I'm constantly aware of him. And not only do I have to think about feeding and changing him, I worry about the logistics of keeping him in view but safe from paint fumes or dust particles."

"I saw the paint you got. It's kid-safe."

"Yes, but I still don't want him breathing in a lot of it. We're becoming a great team. He's a real guy's guy. He was kicking it to the sound of the power tools today."

Nate barked out a laugh and then his gaze turned intense.

"I know I've given you grief, but you've been a lifesaver. I really couldn't have done this without you."

"Thanks. I guess we're a team, too." She shifted her gaze away from the half-naked glory of him to the baby in her arms. Nice guy Nate combined with the fabulous body made him way too appealing.

"Have you thought about what you're going to do when I'm gone?" She pushed the reminder of her looming departure at him along with an internal lecture to take note.

Her goal was to spiff up the house, sell it and move to Los Angeles to get on with her life. She needed to stick to the plan.

Jack chose that moment to smile at her around the nipple in his mouth and he reached out and petted her cheek.

Her insides melted at the trust looking at her from that tiny face. She closed her eyes and pictured L.A.

"I've thought about it." Nate huffed out a frustrated breath in answer to her question about his future plans. "And I talked to Kim. She's given me a list of names to contact for nanny service. She says he's too young for most day-care centers and that they won't take a baby until they're potty-trained."

"A nanny is probably better with your hours anyway."

"True." He propped himself against the doorjamb, his broad frame nearly filling the opening. "It doesn't happen often but there are nights when I'm called out." He gave her a lazy smile. "Fair warning, you might have to cover for me some night."

"Familiar territory," she assured him.

"Right. You would understand. Anyway, it's pretty clear I'm going to need someone to live in."

"I was right, wasn't I? You were think-ing you and Kim could team up to raise the kids. That a wife might be a better bet than a nanny?"

"It crossed my mind." He grimaced. "It wasn't my finest moment."

"No," she agreed. "You both deserve better."

He hung his head, shook it in despair. "I vowed I'd always take care of Kim and Christy. It's the least I can do."

"And I'd say you've met that vow." She carefully removed the bottle. Jack made a few sucking motions and then settled into sleep.

"I'll burp him." Nate came over and gently took Jack. She handed him a receiving blanket to use as a burp cloth and then crossed her legs and unabashedly watched man and baby.

She couldn't help herself. It was like constantly playing with a sore tooth—it wasn't good for you but you couldn't stop doing it.

"Maybe it wouldn't be such a bad solution," she conceded, thinking about his reaction to David. Maybe it was more than protecting his friend's place in her heart. Could Nate be jealous?

"Do you love her?" Something had driven her to ask the question. She shouldn't care. Didn't, she assured herself. It was only for

Jack's sake that she pushed. It wouldn't be fair to him if Nate jumped into a relationship for the wrong reasons.

He went still. The question obviously caught him off guard. And she could see him thinking it through. So what did that mean?

"Yes," he finally declared.

She nodded, not surprised by his response. She knew Kim meant a lot to him, first because of what she'd meant to Quentin, but also from what Kim told her, the two of them had been through a lot together these last few years.

Now the pinch of resentment Michelle felt, *that* surprised her.

She cocked her head, and met him stare for stare. "Do you want her?"

"Ah, hell." No hesitation now, no need to think it through.

She had him. He cared for Kim, but it was clear his feelings for the other woman were no more romantic than hers were for him. And that wasn't going to change.

"So not a solution."

"It was only a passing thought."

"Why did you trade duty with him?"

"What?" Nate alternated rubbing Jack's

back and patting him gently. She found it enthralling to watch his big hands tenderly handle the boy.

"With Quentin," she clarified. "Why did you guys switch duty?"

He sighed. "It was his anniversary and he had a chance to do a video chat with Kim, but it had to be early, so I took his shift."

"So you would have chosen to take that from him?"

He scowled. "Of course not. I knew how much he missed her. How he longed to see his kid."

"If you wouldn't change what led to the two of you being where you were when Quentin got shot, you can't continue to blame yourself."

"Wait." He rubbed a fist over his forehead, as if trying to push the information through. "No. If we hadn't traded—"

"Then Kim wouldn't have those last fond memories of him."

His eyes flashed. "But he'd be alive."

"You don't know that," she said softly. "If you're going to change one element, then other factors could change, as well. The

sniper may have chosen the other target and
Quentin could still be dead."

"No. You're mixing things up."

"I'm saying the only way to change what
happened is to have denied Quentin time with
his wife and daughter. And even then there's
no guarantee he wouldn't still be gone."

Jack burped, the sound loud in the sudden
silence. Nate spent the next few minutes putting Jack back in his bed.

She realized she wasn't going to get an answer. That she'd pressed Nate as far as she
could. She pushed to her feet and walked
to the door, satin sliding sensually over her
body. Halfway through the door she stopped
and glanced at him over her shoulder.

"You're a good guy, Nate. You should give
yourself a break."

CHAPTER NINE

ON Michelle's first day off, she gratefully left Jack in Nate's care, strapped on the tool belt her dad had given her when she was eight and strolled out the front door. The belt felt familiar on her hips and she ran her finger along the notches her dad added to fit her growing figure through the years.

She was supposed to have yesterday off. But it got postponed when the mayor demanded Nate participate in a meeting with the local school district.

Putting aside her annoyance at having her schedule disrespected—she'd expected it, hadn't she—she skipped down the porch steps and strode across the yard.

She'd noticed a couple of fence boards were loose after the storm so she walked the perimeter of the property making repairs where she could and taking notes on boards that needed replacing.

For the front she decided a new coat of paint would do a lot to perk up the curb appeal. Luckily the yard was in good repair because she didn't mind wielding a hammer, but gardening had never been her thing.

Not that Dad hadn't recruited her help there, too. She eyed the early-blooming irises, remembering how helping Dad plant the flower bed around the stone birdbath had earned her freedom from being grounded to go to the Spring Fling Ball with Timothy Smart in junior high. She deemed the dirt under her fingernails a worthwhile payment when Timmy gave her her first kiss at the dance.

Oh, yeah, she had a fondness for irises. She grinned. How Dad would have freaked if he knew. Then she shook her head—who was she kidding? Of course he'd known. He may not have made it to her graduation from junior high to high school, but he always knew what was happening with her. He'd had spies everywhere. It was one of the reasons she'd been so hot to skip town.

With a sigh she walked down the side of the house, along the cement walk her father had

put in when she was all of four or five. Even
then he had her helping him. She remembered
holding the hose over the wheelbarrow while
he mixed the concrete.

At the end of the walk she stopped and
stared down at her tiny handprints imbed-
ded in the cement, her father's large prints
were there, too, on either side of hers. She
remembered how he'd tickled her neck with
his whiskers making her laugh, as he leaned
over her to press his hands in the wet cement.

Now he was gone. There'd be no more projects. Tears stung her eyes and she ran her
finger along the notches again. The tool belt
would be a reminder of her dad for the rest
of her life.

Ten minutes after his shift ended Nate got a
text message from Michelle advising him he'd
invited Kim and David for dinner to thank
them for their help last week and he should
get home as soon as possible.

He'd invited them? No.

Guilt tightened the muscles across his
shoulders as he acknowledged he should have.
Worse, he would have but the whole David

thing continued to annoy him. Kim should have told him she was seeing someone.

Obviously Michelle had picked up his slack and made the arrangements. Not that it was any of her business.

And he told her so thirty minutes later when he confronted her in his kitchen.

"Well, if you would have handled it, I wouldn't have had to," she informed him. "And you're late."

"It's not a nine-to-five job. I was wrapping up a meeting with a neighborhood watch group when I got your text."

"You could have let me know you'd be late." She gave him a chiding glare along with a set of pot holders. "I'm trying to put on a party here. Can you drain the noodles?"

"I didn't ask for a party. Kim is my friend. She knows I'm grateful for the furniture. I already told her so." He dumped the noodles into the colander, turning his face away from the rising steam.

He noticed she'd hung new curtains. Gone were the dull white ruffles and in their place a soft yellow wafted in the light breeze. They looked fresh and clean against the crisp white of the newly painted trim.

"Oh? So you've talked to her since they delivered the furniture?"

"Well, no." He set the pan back on the stove. "Come on. Friends don't have to keep repeating themselves."

"Not usually, but this was a big favor and it involved more than Kim. You barely know David and he put in a big effort."

Replacing Nate at the stove, she pulled another pan forward and lifted the lid. The scents of garlic and bacon filled the air.

"Him." He used his hip to push her aside and lifted the heavy pan to pour the contents over the noodles. "This looks great. What is it?"

"Yes, David. Kim cares for him." She edged in next to him and began to fold the creamy mixture into the noodles. "If you care for Kim like you say you do, you'll make an effort with David. It's spaghetti carbonara."

He licked a finger. "Tasty."

"Glad you like it. You can set the table."

"I'll tell you what I don't like." He opened the cupboard with the plates. "David."

"You don't know him. This dinner will help remedy that."

Catching her looking at him from the corner of her emerald eyes Nate braced himself for what was coming. He'd already revealed way too much to her the other night. Sitting there in a pink little bit of nothing that clung to her curves as faithfully as a lover, she'd raked him over the coals both emotionally and physically.

"She told me you're like a brother to her."

"Yeah," he admitted with no small sense of relief, "which doesn't make it any easier to see her with David."

"She deserves to be loved, Nate. After all she's suffered, she deserves to be happy. You want that for her, don't you? And for her to be taken care of? Isn't that what Quentin would want for her?"

God, she had his number. Knew just what keys to tap. And she was right about all of it. He wanted Kim and Christy to have everything they needed and wanted. Whether it was him to give it to them or not.

"David makes her happy," Michelle said in a whisper as if the softness would make it easier to accept. And then she turned brisk. "Never mind the table. I've got the rest of this. You should go change if you plan to. They'll be here in fifteen minutes. Oh, and I invited Dolly, too."

"Of course," he muttered as he left the room. "The more the merrier."

Actually Dolly was a great addition to the party. It gave him someone to talk to other than David.

Michelle picked up the plates and followed Nate from the room, watching as he jogged up the stairs. He moved with a lithe grace that was a pure joy to see.

But he was totally off-limits. She'd lectured herself severely on staying detached. This whole dinner party was just an excuse to talk to Dolly.

This morning it had finally clicked with Michelle, duh, that if Nate was renting the house, he must be paying rent. When she asked where he was sending the payments to, he told her Dolly because that was where he had been sending it and he'd never been notified to send it anywhere else.

Dolly was a retired attorney. It stood to reason she'd know where the money was. Michelle should have thought about her dad's affairs before now. She knew he didn't own much beyond the house and a truck older than she was, but there may be something she should take care of.

Michelle liked Dolly. She and Dad had been friends forever. But Michelle didn't know what to think about her dad and Dolly hooking up. It was just such a foreign concept for Michelle to think of him in that way. Anyway, she preferred this meeting with the woman be informal.

So far so good. The carbonara was a hit. Nate actually appeared to be giving David a fair shake, helped along by Dolly's easy chatter. Christy was enthralled with Jack and wanted to treat him like a doll, but otherwise so far so good.

The chill brought on by the storm a week ago was gone, replaced by the warm days of spring. With both the front and back doors open a breeze blew through the house making it easy for them to linger at the table.

Now came the hard part. They'd all carried their plates into the kitchen and the others were headed for the living room. It was Michelle's chance to get the older woman alone.

"Dolly, would you like to see the work I've done refurbishing my dad's old rocking chair?"

"Sure." The petite, white-haired woman turned at Michelle's invitation. "I don't remember him having a rocker."

"We found it in the attic when we went looking for baby furniture. None of my baby stuff was there. I'm kind of surprised the rocker was. Dad believed in use it or lose it."

"That's exactly how he was." Dolly laughed. "I swear if I didn't eat fast enough, half my meal ended up in the trash."

"He was always after me to eat, so he didn't do that to me. But I did have to explain to a teacher once that he'd thrown my homework away."

"Oh, goodness." Dolly's brown eyes danced with mirth. "That ranks right up there with the dog eating it."

"Exactly." Feeling justified even after all these years, Michelle led the way into the garage. "The teacher wouldn't let me make it up until I had my dad call him and admit he'd trashed it."

Laughing together, she met Dolly's gaze and suddenly her throat swelled up and tears filled her eyes. She swallowed and blinked, seeking control. Instead the tears overflowed and rained down her cheeks.

She missed her dad.

While she was in San Francisco it hadn't been so bad, probably because she was used to being alone there. She'd had her friends, especially Amanda, but her dad had little to do with her life in the city. He'd visit a couple of times a year, always made a point to come to her gigs. And she'd always been so proud when he sat in the audience.

Coming home and not finding Dad here felt wrong. The situation with Nate and Jack kept her busy and distracted, but the truth was she kept expecting to see her dad, to run into him when she entered a room.

Of course she didn't. Not physically, but there was evidence of him everywhere.

She tried to pretend she was fine, because if she pretended hard enough eventually she really would be fine. It was hard, though,

"Oh, my dear." Dolly's arms wrapped her in sympathy, in comfort. "I miss him, too. Every day."

They stood, tears flowing, locked together in love and sorrow for a man gone but not forgotten, who'd been important to each of them in different ways.

After a few minutes, Michelle pulled away,

walked to the workbench and brought back a box of tissues. She offered a couple to Dolly.

"Thank you." The older woman mopped her eyes and dabbed at her nose. She looked dewy but none the worse for wear.

Michelle knew her eyes were red-rimmed and her nose rivaled Rudolph's, but she pushed the notion aside.

"I've been so mad at him," she confessed.

"Oh, my dear. Why?"

"For not telling me he was sick." She plucked at the damp tissue. "I could have spent more time with him if I'd known. Made him take better care of himself."

"After his scare, he did change his diet and begin exercising more. He was trying."

More tears leaked out. "I never thought of us as being that close. He was always rushing off to take care of business. And the distance just got worse when I moved to the city."

"Oh, sweetheart. I loved your father, but when it came to expressing his emotions, he was a complete cotton head. You don't want to know how long it took him to kiss me the first time."

Michelle threw up a staying hand.

"No, I really don't." She confirmed with a

half-hysterical laugh. "That's not a picture I want in my head."

"Of course," Dolly said with a bit of a twinkle. "What I'm trying to say is he may not have said so often, but he loved you very much."

Michelle shook her head and tossed the used tissues in a bin at the end of the workbench. Not often?

Try rare as fairy dust.

She'd only ever heard him say those three little words once a year on her birthday, and then only when he thought she was asleep. She heard it for the first time when she was eight. Every birthday after that, she'd pretended to be asleep early, just to hear the words.

"With Mom gone, it was just the two of us. We should have been tight. But—"

"He put you second." Dolly nodded, her well-defined brows puckered in a frown. "I saw it as you were growing up. It's one of the few things we argued about. It was his self-defense mechanism after your mom died. He needed work and the sense of duty to help him cope, to give him focus. He genuinely couldn't see what it was doing to you."

Choked up, Michelle stared at her feet, focusing on the black sneakers with the bright pink trim. She frowned at a white smudge of paint on the toe.

"He was the job."

"Yes, beyond anything else, he was the job. But I also know it hurt him to know he failed you."

"He didn't fail me," she insisted. "I learned to cope, too. And I knew if I truly needed him, he'd be there for me."

"I'm glad you realize that." Dolly's smile was sad. "He had his way, you know, of showing his love. Taking out the trash without being asked. Handling little fix-its around the house before they became big fix-its. Drawing me into projects so we spent time together."

Michelle thought of the reminders of her dad she'd found while updating the house to sell, how she kept coming across projects he insisted they work on together. She thought of her tool belt and swallowed hard.

Yes, that was exactly his way.

"I want him back."

"Me, too." Dolly kissed Michelle's cheek.

"We'll just have to keep him close in our hearts. Now, where is that rocking chair?"

"Rocking chair?" Michelle blanked for a minute, and then remembered her gambit to get Dolly alone. She still needed to talk to the woman about her father's affairs. She hadn't meant to get so emotional.

"It's over here." She hit the button to lift the garage door and let in the light, then led Dolly to where the mission-style rocker sat on a tarp on the far side of the garage.

"I've stripped it, sanded the treads until they were even and used wood glue to tighten the dowels. Now it's ready to be stained."

"Oh, my dear. You've done a wonderful job. This is a beautiful piece." She sighed. "And I know why your dad kept it."

"Really?" Surprised, Michelle demanded, "Why? How?"

"Your father had a picture of this chair in his things. It's of you and your mother. She's holding you against her shoulder and you're both asleep. It's very Madonna-like."

"Oh." The vision left Michelle speechless.

"It's beautiful. And was obviously a prized possession of your father's."

"Can I have the picture?"

"Of course." Dolly squeezed her hands. "I have all his things for you. And we can go over his estate whenever you're ready."

"His estate? I didn't think he had anything besides the house. I was just going to ask after the rent for this place."

"There's that, yes. But your father lived simply and saved. He had a college fund for you that you never used. And of course there was his life insurance, which has been placed in an account for you at his bank."

"I had no idea." Stunned, Michelle's mind whirled. She'd pulled into town with the last of her savings in her pocket and a desperate plan to turn it into a nest egg to finance a new life in Los Angeles.

It never occurred to her Dad had any assets beyond the house. The windfall was bittersweet, she could use the money, but it came at such a high price.

"I'm sorry." Dolly's voice trembled a little. "I should have made a better attempt to talk to you at the funeral, but it was such a difficult time for me."

"Stop." Michelle hugged the woman. "I understand. Tell me the rest."

"I tried to reach you afterward, but the contact information I found was no longer good."

Michelle grimaced, remembering the loss of yet another job, of having to mooch off Amanda while she tried to find something new in an ever shrinking job market.

"It was a difficult time for me, too."

"I'd like to hear about it," Dolly said with sincerity. "Why don't you come over some day this week? We can talk and I can give you your dad's things."

Michelle had been so reluctant going into this meeting but at the end she felt closer to both her father and Dolly.

She nodded. "I'd like that."

"So you're serious about this David guy?" Nate followed Kim to a small SUV parked at the curb. She'd brought another box of baby things and he'd volunteered to carry them inside.

Michelle's instincts appeared to be on target where Kim and David were concerned, but he wanted to hear it from Kim.

"Come on, Nate. He's not that 'David guy.' You two have met a couple of times. He's a well-respected member of the community."

She popped her trunk and then stood back so he could reach the box.

"Huh." In no hurry, he leaned a hip against the dark green vehicle and crossed his arms over his chest. "We've bumped into each other at a few events. But I don't know the man."

"Considering your occupation, that's a good thing." Both her tone and posture challenged.

He had to concede her point. And her defense of David indicated her emotions were engaged.

Seemed emotions were on the playbill today. From where he stood he saw Michelle and Dolly wrapped together with the waterworks flowing. A frown drew his brows together. It wasn't like Michelle to get all weepy.

"Nate." Kim called his name and he shifted his gaze to her.

"Yeah."

"I want you to give David a chance," she implored him. "He's important to me."

"I see." Well, there was his confirmation. He flicked a glance toward the garage. Michelle had been right. She appeared more composed and he nodded.

"I'm glad you understand." Kim wrapped him in a hug. "You're important to me, too. In a different way."

He patted her on the back. "I'll always be here if you need me."

"I know you don't have to be." She stepped back and gave him a watery smile. "But you will be. You were a good friend to Quentin."

"I'm your friend, too."

"Yes. But you came here and helped me and Christy because of him. I'm not too proud to say we needed you. That I was glad for your help even though you owed us nothing."

He shoved his hands in his pockets and looked away. Michelle and Dolly were inspecting the rocker.

"I wouldn't say nothing."

"I would," Kim insisted. "Quentin was a soldier to the bone, he knew the drill, accepted the risks. We both did. He wouldn't have wanted you to take a bullet because of his choices."

"It's not fair. He had a wife and child. Nobody would have missed me."

"Oh, my God, Nate." Kim pushed the strawberry-blond hair away from her face

with both hands. "That is so not true. I hope
you don't believe that."

"It's true enough," he argued gruffly. "Nobody depended on me like you depended on
Quentin."

"Your cousin Jack needed you. He would
have been lost without you."

"Not even Jack could help Jack."

"But you did. He tried because of you."

"I didn't do him any favors. He joined the
service because of me. And the war killed
him, in a slow and painful process."

"Stop it this instant. You are not responsible for the decisions other people make. War
is hell. It breaks the strong and the weak.
Jack loved you. He respected you. And he
deserves your respect in return." Impassioned
she pointed toward the house. "And if you
want to talk about someone needing you, let's
talk about Jack's son."

"Okay." He pulled her in for a fierce hug.
"Settle down."

"Let me go." She pushed away, fire flash-
ing in her blue eyes. "I won't listen to you
bad-mouth yourself. You're one of the best
men I know and no one gets to trash talk my
friend, not even you."

"All right. You win." Unable to meet her gaze he stared at the toes of his boots. "I'm wonderful."

"Darn right," she snapped, clearly unappeased. "Now say it with a little more conviction. You talk some sense into him. I'm done trying."

Nate looked up to see whose mercy Kim had tossed him to and saw Michelle stood on the curb a few feet away. Why would Kim think Michelle had any sway over him?

He wondered how much she'd heard. Not that it mattered. She pretty much poked her little nose wherever she wanted.

Kim reached into the back of the SUV and lifted the box out. He held out his hands but she walked right by him.

"Hey, I thought I was carrying that."

"That was before I was mad at you. Now I can get it myself." She jutted her chin and narrowed her eyes at him. "And make friends with David, you big lug. You'll like each other if you give it half a chance."

She stormed up the walk and David came out when she reached the porch and took the box. Great.

With a sigh Nate closed the rear door of the

SUV. Michelle came over and leaned against it next to him.

"I'll never understand women."

"That's because you're a man and you have to complicate things."

"Me? She's mad because I said Quentin should be here instead of me."

"She's mad because you devalued yourself. And if your life means nothing, does that mean the last three years spent helping her mean nothing?"

"Of course not."

"You blame yourself for both Quentin's and Jack's deaths, but have you ever thought that by taking responsibility you're robbing them of their dignity?"

Appalled, he shook his head. "I'd never do that."

"Life is a series of decisions, actions and consequences. They put us in a certain place at a certain time and life happens. Sometimes you meet that special someone. Or make the deal of a lifetime. Or you could die. Jack struggled in the end, but the same man that raised you raised him. I have to believe at one point he was a strong, capable man. As was Quentin. By honoring their choices you honor their memories."

"Kim said something like that." He rubbed a hand around the back of his neck. He felt like he'd been put through the spin cycle. First Kim and then Michelle questioned his motives when he was just trying to do his best.

Funny how when Kim talked to him, his defenses crackled, but Michelle had a way of offering him options that empowered him.

"Smart woman. You should listen to her." She punched him in the arm and headed inside. After a few steps, she stopped and waved him along. "Come on. We're having ice-cream floats for dessert."

He followed her retreat with brooding eyes.

He had all the respect in the world for Jack and Quentin. But how was he supposed to shrug off their deaths when they seemed so pointless? And when they'd had so much to live for?

Still he needed to think about what Michelle and Kim were saying because he'd rather cut off his right arm than do anything to dishonor Quentin or Jack.

His cell buzzed in his pocket. He fished the phone out and flipped it open. A couple of minutes later, he went inside to make his excuses. He'd have to miss out on the ice-cream floats. There'd been an incident at Pete's Hardware and Nate had to go.

Luckily he escaped before he had to admit the women were right.

CHAPTER TEN

A WEEK later Michelle slowly rocked Jack as he took his bottle at 2:00 a.m. Tonight was Nate's turn, but he'd been called out to an accident on the main highway.

Her muscles ached with each motion of the chair. She'd finished painting the castle today. It looked great—soft lavender with white trim, a true castle in the sky.

She was a little surprised she was still here. As they'd planned, she'd met up with Dolly for lunch earlier in the week. Her dad had provided well for her in his death. She should have known he would, because he'd provided well for her in life, physically if not emotionally.

Excited, her immediate reaction was to take the money and run, waving to River Run via her rearview mirror.

And then she left the meeting and had her

first hesitation when she strapped Jack into his car seat. How could she think of leaving him? He'd already lost his father and his mother. Yes, he loved Nate, the two of them were as close as a dog and his bone, but losing someone else would no doubt affect his little psyche.

Not to mention Nate had yet to find a sitter or nanny to take her place.

He'd allowed her to stay and start on the house in exchange for helping with Jack. Nate had needed the help, but so had she and he'd come through for her.

And truthfully living with him wasn't so bad. Sure his schedule could be erratic, but she'd also arrived home from running errands or visiting Kim to find Nate had started dinner or folded the laundry. They'd fallen into a rhythm and it worked.

Sure her circumstances had changed but she still needed to deal with selling the house. If she left now, she'd just have to come back to finish what she'd started. Once she got to Los Angeles she wanted to concentrate on the future, not be drawn back to the past.

Better to stay and see it through now.

Jack whimpered. Poor guy was in a bit of a

mood tonight. She began to hum and when he opened his eyes to look at her she sang softly.

My American man opens his arms, opens
his home
To a fatherless child, lost and alone.
He heats up the bottle, rocks him to and fro.
My American man is an everyday hero.

Jack smiled and her heart lurched. Yeah, here was the true reason she was staying. And oh, she had it bad.

She sang a while longer playing with the words to a song she'd been working on and he slid into sleep. She kissed him softly and put him in his crib, and then lingered for a moment, tucking the blanket around him, making sure he was sleeping soundly.

With a sigh, she turned to leave and found Nate standing in the doorway watching her. She stopped, caught by something in his expression. He looked tired, but more than that he looked tormented. And she knew it must have been bad tonight.

That he was in need tonight.

Again her heart lurched. Oh, man. She

knew better than to let him close, to allow him in. That wasn't why she was staying.

But the pain in his eyes cut through all that.

"Hey," she said softly.

Without a word he walked to her, cupped her face in his hands and took her mouth with his. She tasted his desperation, his need, and gave him everything he craved, going on her toes to get closer to him.

He groaned and wrapped his arms around her, hugging her near and deepening the kiss. For long moments he ravaged her mouth, stealing her breath and her senses.

She thrilled to his touch, to the heat building between them. Inching closer she pressed her body to his, aligning thigh to thigh, hip to hip, breast to chest. Oh, yeah.

He lifted his head, pressed his forehead to hers. Breath ragged, he demanded, "My bed or yours?"

"I have a twin." She imagined the two of them squeezed onto the small bed and thought it wouldn't be such a bad thing. But bigger would be better.

"Mine then." He took her hand and turned for the door.

"The master has a king."

A smoldering glance pinned her over his shoulder. "Too much space."

Yeah, plus she really needed to make changes in there before she'd be comfortable thinking of it as anything other than Dad's room.

To prove she liked how Nate thought she pushed him through his door and followed him inside. Closing it behind her, she leaned back against wood. A quick glance confirmed Nate's baby monitor was active on his nightstand. Good.

Biting her lower lip in a sexy moue, she beckoned to him. His eyes blazed with desire, and he prowled back to her. Placing both hands on the wooden barrier either side of her head, he lowered his head and claimed her mouth with his. He ran his tongue along the seam of her mouth and softly nipped her bottom lip, punishing her for taunting him.

Or rewarding her.

"Ouch." She sighed. And then returned the favor, using her teeth on him, and rejoiced in his groan of need. Circling his neck with her arms, she allowed him to carry her to his bed, to lower her to her feet. "More." She threaded her fingers in his hair and pulled him to her for another heated kiss.

"This is probably a bad idea," she said when they came up for air. And then, her eyes on his, she slipped the straps of her cotton camisole off her shoulders. Anticipation flaring in his gaze, he hooked his thumbs in the sides and pushed the garment down her body, catching the waist of her pajama shorts along the way.

"Oh, I'm sure we'll regret it," he agreed, nibbling on her ear. "But I don't want to stop. Do you?"

"You could try to stop." Shivering under his intent stare, she reached for the buttons of his uniform. "But I'd hate to have to hurt you so early in our relationship."

He laughed. But he shook his head and stopped her. Instead he swept the covers back, letting them fall off the end, and then he pushed her gently down.

"No danger of that." He assured her, making quick work of stripping off his clothes. And lowering himself next to her.

He went to kiss her but she placed a finger against his lips to halt him. He nipped her finger then lifted a dark brow in question.

"Are you sure you wouldn't rather talk?"

"You're kidding me, right?"

"You're obviously upset from the accident."

"It was a fatality. Two dead, a child and his mother. I really don't want to talk about watching a man lose his family. I want to forget." He dipped his head and did something with his mouth that made lightning sing through her body.

"Make me forget," he said against her skin.

"Forget what?" She gasped, already lost under the skill of his hands and lips, arching as he played her like a delicate instrument.

She wrapped herself around him, giving, taking, wondering. From one moment to the next caress became demand, became the need for more, for harder, deeper, higher until she bowed under the exquisite flow of sensation. With a cry she clung to him, her ballast in the storm, and soared with him through the night.

Jack's soft whimpering woke Nate the next morning. Instantly alert, he opened his eyes to see it was before seven. No need for the woman in his arms to be up yet. God, she felt good against him, soft and warm and female. How could something that felt so right, be so wrong?

He kissed the bare curve of her shoulder and eased away from the temptation of her. Pulling on his jeans he crossed the hall to tend Jack.

"Hi, buddy." He greeted the baby. At the sound of his voice Jack stopped whimpering and smiled. "Sorry I missed your feeding last night. It couldn't be avoided."

He'd been feeling raw when he'd gotten home last night. Death was never easy. And the Lord knew Nate had seen more than his fair share of it. But it's not something a guy became accustomed to. At least he hoped he never got that callous.

He'd asked Michelle to help him forget. And she had helped. He hadn't truly forgotten, the victims deserved better than that, but she'd given him the distance he needed to cope with the memories.

Finding her standing over Jack dressed in a skimpy T-shirt and shorts, singing softly to the baby about everyday heroes, instantly relieved his distress. Her sensual beauty and sweet voice soothed him, the perfect foil for the devastation he'd come from.

Every day he fought the need to taste her again, to feel her in his arms. He understood she didn't fit in his life, that when she got the money from the house she'd be gone in a blink.

Last night, he hadn't cared.

Need overrode common sense and in the wee hours of a difficult night, he'd been drawn across the room, compelled to inhale her scent, to surround himself in her warmth. And her eager response eased his troubled soul.

He lifted Jack from his bed, made quick work of changing his diaper and carried him downstairs to prep his bottle. While the formula heated in the microwave, Nate got the coffee going.

He amazed himself with how adept he'd become with the routine. He should thank Michelle for that, too. She was so impressed with his decision to take in Jack, Nate hated the thought of looking like a freaked-out pansy handling the baby—which was how he'd really felt—so he'd faked it.

Reading instructions on the formula can, total pansy, making note of how the snaps and tapes and buckles went as he undid them so he could put them back. Watching Michelle, seeing how she did things. He'd been a total cheat. But it had worked. Now he only occasionally freaked out.

Jack squeaked and shifted to look at the microwave, a clue to Nate he'd missed hearing the bell.

He grinned at Jack. "I'll tell you this—" he lifted the boy so they met eye to eye "—my head may be all over the place, but I feel great."

"I'm feeling pretty good myself," Michelle drawled from the doorway.

He tucked Jack against his shoulder and met her gaze across the width of the room. "Hey."

"Good morning." She strolled over, circled his neck with one arm and kissed him softly. With a sigh she pulled away and walked to the coffeemaker to pour herself a cup of the strong brew.

"What's wrong with your head?" she asked after her first sip.

Jack began to protest the delay of his breakfast, so Nate pulled the baby's bottle from the microwave and fed it to him before responding.

She smelled of soap and a hint of mint and looked beautiful without a speck of makeup. His body tightened as images of her in his arms woke up his libido.

Forget Wheaties, the breakfast of champions stood in front of him, her sweet butter hair, cherry lips and peaches-and-cream skin made her look good enough to eat.

Oh, yeah, he wanted him some for breakfast.

Too bad all that sweetness was bad for him.

And he still had night mouth.

"I was messed up last night." Definitely not thinking straight. And her kiss just sent his morning ricocheting off course. What did it mean? "You helped. Thanks."

Was it a morning-after kiss? Or was it a she-thought-they'd-started-something kiss?

"A fatality must be difficult to deal with. Especially a child," she sympathized.

"You know, hold that thought." He pushed Jack into her arms. "And Jack. I'll be right back."

Either way she meant the kiss, he didn't want the final marker of last night to be a mere peck on the mouth. Not when it was going to have to last him a lifetime.

He shot upstairs, hit the bathroom for a quick spit and shine, grabbed a shirt and headed back downstairs.

In the kitchen he rewrote history. Jack played with a rattle in the portable crib under the window and Michelle whisked something at the counter.

Grabbing her hand he whirled her into his arms and captured her mouth with his in a lover's kiss, swift and needy, a dance of tongues in a heated embrace. He drowned himself in her, sipping from the minty freshness of her lips.

He lifted his head once, but it was too soon. So he shifted to a new angle and sank into her again. And she was right there with him. She climbed onto his feet, lifted onto her toes and took him prisoner by circling him in her arms, surrendering to the passion consuming them.

The need to breathe broke them apart. Forehead to forehead he sawed for air as if he'd run a four-minute mile. She sighed and swayed into him. He had to set his knees to hold them up. He buried his nose in her hair, breathed deep of sunshine and hibiscus.

She turned her head and bit him on the arm.

"Ow!" He set her at arm's length. "What the hell?"

"My thought exactly." She threw back her head and propped her hands on her hips. "I know goodbye when it smacks me in the mouth. I shouldn't be surprised. You said you'd have regrets."

"But I don't," he denied.

"Looks like boo-hoo from where I'm standing."

The woman donned attitudes like other women wore accessories. Different occasions requiring different 'tudes. He saw just enough hurt in her defiant eyes to recognize her attack as a defensive move.

Fine. She wanted a fight?

He got right up in her grill. "No regrets." He made it clear. "Not a single one. You were the best time I've ever had."

"You bet your derriere I am."

She didn't blink. Didn't back down an inch, which was seriously hot. And an unwanted distraction.

He bit back a smile, knowing any show of amusement would only antagonize her more.

"I'm not a gambling man."

Her vibrant green eyes narrowed suspiciously.

"But?"

"No buts."

"Seriously?"

"There were no promises made. None inferred." This close to her, with the air sizzling between them, he almost regretted that. "We're both adults who know the score."

"Yet it won't happen again." It was a statement, which told him she'd come to the same conclusion.

"It's for the best."

Each breath brought her scent into him until he longed to eliminate the space between them. Instead he carefully stepped back.

"Don't you agree?"

"Yes." An odd twitch of her head accompanied the agreement and then she swung around and picked up the whisk. "It's for the best."

She beat furiously at the poor concoction in the bowl.

He ached to go to her, to pull her stiff body into his and re-create the magic they'd made last night. But good as it had been there was no future in it.

And he knew in that moment why none of the women he'd interviewed for Jack's nanny were working out. None of them were Michelle.

Until he worked that out, he needed her help with Jack. It wouldn't be smart to get involved with her in any other capacity. Not for such a short amount of time.

Not when he was already half in love with her.

CHAPTER ELEVEN

It was her own fault, Michelle bemoaned as she bounced Jack on her hip and watched three little girls play ring-around-the-rosie with the coffee table. She allowed Kim and Dolly to gang up on her.

It took all her energy and ingenuity to take care of one little boy. What made them—or her—think she could take on four kids at one time?

The thing was Dolly and Kim were friends with two of Michelle's old classmates who had opened an internet cupcake pop business. It was a good news-bad news scenario. Good news for her classmates' business, bad news for Michelle, who was called on to babysit while everyone baked, dipped and shipped.

"Girls, let's head outside. I have apples and oranges for everyone."

As the girls shrieked their excitement, she ushered them outside.

No doubt about it, she'd gotten the rough end of the arrangement. She'd been looking forward to four o'clock, when the moms were supposed to pick up their young. That was before the phone call saying they needed another hour. Or two!

Nate was going to freak when he got home.

"Castle." Awe colored Christy's voice and lit up her big blue eyes as she took in the refurbished tree house. "I wanna go in the castle."

"Castle, castle." The other girls began to chant. They were all under four.

"Oh, no. No. No. No." Michelle tried to stop the stampede of three-year-olds, but it was no contest. They almost knocked her off her feet. She hugged Jack to her and prayed for a miracle.

"Girls, I can't take the baby up there and you can't go alone. Girls!" She glanced helplessly at the table and then back at the heads bobbing around the base of the tree. "There's fruit."

Giving up, she crossed the lawn at a trot,

catching Christy around the waist and lifting her off the ladder leading up.

"Sorry, kids, but you're too small."

Too small and too many for her to handle on her own while also taking care of Jack.

The wailing started.

The girls scattered like cats after pigeons, each trying to get to the ladder when she chased another away. Delighted with the game, Jack giggled. Not so thrilled, Michelle growled under her breath.

"Stop. I said stop." Her stern tone had no impact on the tiny tots. Their merry shrieks were loud enough to pierce the eardrum.

"What's going on out here?" a male voice demanded.

Of course Nate was early. You could never count on a lawman's schedule. Late when you wanted them home, early when you needed extra time. But today she didn't care.

She swung around and found the sight of Nate standing on the back patio such a sight for frazzled nerves her standoffish attitude of the last two weeks vanished in an instant.

Rushing to his side, she thrust Jack into his arms.

"I'm never having kids," she announced.

And turned back to corral the girls. She shook her head as she saw Christy was halfway up the ladder again. Definitely the instigator in this crowd.

Nate quickly passed Michelle, moving Jack into one arm and snagging Christy safely with his other. He blocked the ladder so the other little girls couldn't get up and turned to face Michelle, the two children perched smugly in his embrace, obviously unfazed by his stern demeanor.

"I asked what was going on."

Happy for a moment's respite, Michelle plopped down in a patio chair, grabbed an apple slice and bit off the end. Flavor exploded in her mouth, the sweetness and crunch as satisfying as the joy of handing over authority. Even if it only lasted for a brief moment.

"Where's Mama?" Christy asked.

"Good question," Nate told her. His gaze pinned Michelle. "Spill."

With a sigh she filled him in on the whole babysitting gig.

"How long ago did Kim call?"

She glanced at her watch. "An hour and a half."

The corner of his mouth lifted in a grim half smile and he pulled his cell out of his pocket.

"Hey," he said into the phone. "Your daughter is asking for you." Pause. "No, I'm not early. How's it going over there?" He listened for a few minutes, throwing in an occasional grunt. "How much longer do you think that's going to take? Another hour and a half?"

Michelle's heart sank. She threw up both hands in a staying motion and frantically shook her head. After five hours, she was more than ready to throw in the towel. In fact, give her a towel—a bubble bath sounded really good right about now.

Listening to him agree to additional time, she thought she better get some cupcake pops out of this or someone would pay.

"I can't believe you caved," she groused when he hung up. "Chump."

He laughed and set Christy down to play with her friends. "You started it."

"Last time I make that mistake," she assured him. It was good to hear him laugh again. The last couple of weeks had been very stiff between them. She'd missed him. "I thought I was such hot stuff because I've been taking care of Jack. But he's sweet and happy, and quiet. I'm telling you these girls are from a whole other planet."

"Michelle." He was totally patronizing.

"And they don't talk on their planet. They scream."

"You're tired."

"Completely wiped."

"Uncle Nate." Christy tugged on his pant leg. "We want to go in the castle."

"Yeah." The other two girls cheered. "We want to go in the castle!"

"That's their latest thing, but they can't go up alone and I couldn't help them and hold Jack, too." She waved to the fruit on the table. "I made them a snack. But I brought them out here and now all they're interested in is the castle."

"Well, they are little girls."

"Yeah."

"And you did spiff it up so it looks pretty enchanting."

"Yeah, it's pretty dope." He was trying to butter her up, and darned if it wasn't working.

"Well, we have the girls for another hour or more." Without shifting his attention from her, he carefully removed his badge from Jack's grasp and tucked it in his pants pocket. "Why don't we add some sandwiches and have a picnic in the *c-a-s-t-l-e*."

She perked up in an instant. She loved the idea. A tea party in the castle, how perfect. It had been way too long since she played princess.

"Excellent." She popped up, threw her arms around him, kissed him on the cheek and Jack on the mouth. "Tiaras! We're going to need tiaras."

"Hold it," Nate called after her as she skipped into the house. "We are not playing dress-up."

She simply wiggled her fingers at him over her shoulder. Of course they were playing dress-up. Why hadn't she thought of it sooner?

In her room she found everything she needed.

For all his quickness to toss clutter, her dad had left her room pretty much alone. After her conversations with Dolly, Michelle began to see signs of his affection all over the house. Here was another. And her heart warmed as she headed for the closet.

Since she'd always been a princess in her

heart she had plenty of fluff and frills from the past. In her zest to clean things out she'd bagged most of it for Goodwill, so she knew right where to go.

She dumped the bag on the bed, plucked out the items they couldn't use and a couple of things with sharp edges and put the rest back in the bag. Draping a pink boa around her neck, she grabbed the bag and hurried downstairs.

In the kitchen Jack was in the portable crib, the girls sat like perfect angels at the table— yeah, she believed that—and Nate stood in front of the open refrigerator. She grabbed the grape jelly from the door and handed it to him.

"Three peanut-butter-and-jelly sandwiches cut into four triangles each," she instructed him. "And then can you find a box or a basket we can use to carry all the food?"

"Sure."

Ten minutes later they packed his sandwiches along with the ham-and-cheese she'd made, the sliced fruit, cookies, water, soda and juice packs into a huge basket.

"Ready," she announced and handed the food to Nate to carry.

"Yeah!" The girls clapped and jumped from their seats to follow him outside.

Michelle picked up Jack and then decided to detour by the living room for the throw and some pillows.

"Am I going to fit up there?" Nate demanded when she caught up with them at the ladder of the tree house.

She eyed his broad shoulders and had a moment's doubt. But she looked up and saw the opening and figured it might be tight, but he'd make it.

"My dad did, so you should," she assured him.

She went first and laid out the blanket and pillows, and then Nate handed her Jack and she tucked him between two of the pillows. Next the girls climbed up one at a time. And finally Nate joined them.

Instantly the spacious six-by-nine-foot room shrank to dollhouse proportions. Man, he was huge. And totally out of place at a princess tea party.

Yet here he was. And after they'd spent the last two weeks avoiding each other. He sat with his back to the wall, legs drawn up in front of him. The man was all male, all the time. The Lord knew she'd had a heck of a time pretending he didn't exist.

And yet he let Christy and her friends dress him up for the tea party. They wrapped a gauzy scarf around his neck, beads around his thick wrist and put stickers on his boots.

The pained expression on his face spoke volumes. And still he accepted a tiny sandwich triangle on a pink napkin as if Michelle offered him a gourmet treat.

"Thanks." He devoured the triangle in one bite. "I have to say I'm impressed with the job you did on this tree house. I was ready to tear it down."

She threw him a chiding glare as she wrapped a sparkling pink necklace around a headband. "It was weathered but it's built well. A few nails and a fresh coat of paint was all it needed."

"You're making it sound easier than it was. You're such a girly girl, how do you even know how to do all the home repair stuff?"

"My dad." She put the makeshift tiara on Christy's head and pulled her fine brown hair free of the headband. "He was always dragging me into helping on some project or another. Building, plumbing, gardening—we did all kinds of stuff. Everything but electrical. I only got to watch him do electrical."

"That's actually smart. Electrical can be dangerous."

Christy preened and posed for the other two girls and they crowded closer, wanting tiaras of their own. Michelle reached for the shimmering blue beads and a plastic purple headband.

"Yeah, it didn't hurt my feelings not to mess with electricity."

"I suppose not."

"Dolly said drawing me into working with him was Dad's way of showing his love. Working on the house, seeing all the different projects we worked on together, it's like I've found him again."

"Then it's a good thing you came back."

Tears burned at the back of her eyes. She blinked them away, determined to keep them happy memories.

"Yes." She met his gaze. "I'm glad I came."

Red crystals woven through a soft cream scarf and wrapped around blond pigtails made up the last tiara. The girls giggled and practiced bowing to each other.

Michelle laughed and pulled out the plate

she'd tucked into the bottom of the basket. Loading it with sandwiches, fruit and cookies, she handed it to Nate with both hands.

His eyes lit up and he eagerly reached for it. She held on to to the edge until he looked up with a question on his face.

"Thank you," she told him. "This is special for them. For me. We couldn't have done it without you."

He winked. "Just call me Prince Charming."

"Today has been so great," Amanda told Michelle as they settled at an outdoor table in a café on the wharf. "I'm going to miss you heaps when you move to Los Angeles. Promise you'll visit often."

"Now that I have some funds, you can bet I will. Los Angeles doesn't even seem real to me yet. It's going to be tough. And lonely."

"Elle is just down the road in San Diego. She's excited about your move. And this song is a winner, Mich. If you sent it to the record companies instead of the artists, they'd snap you up in a heartbeat."

"I'm a behind-the-scenes girl. Have been ever since that first year at Princess Camp."

Amanda rolled her eyes. "Most people get over stage fright."

Michelle just shook her head and ignored the years-long disagreement. The waiter came and went with their coffee order.

"You really think it will sell?" She bit her lip. "Everyday Hero" was so close to her heart, she had no objectivity on this one.

"I do." Amanda squeezed her hand in encouragement. "He sounds pretty special. Tell me about him."

Michelle hesitated; she was usually the one in control of her relationships. She never had trouble walking away. This time it didn't feel so easy. With a sigh she spilled her guts, telling Amanda all about Nate and Jack, and of finding peace with her father's memory.

"Girl, you are in trouble," Amanda declared after a sip of latte.

"I know. It feels like I'm a different person now than when I moved to River Run two months ago. I still want to succeed with my music, but the overwhelming desire to get to Los Angeles has eased up."

"Do you love him?"

"Jack? Yeah. He's such a sweetheart I defy anyone not to love him."

"You're so full of it. You know who I mean. If you care about this guy, maybe you should give it a chance."

"He's a cop, he lives in River Run, and he has enough baggage to fill a jumbo jet. Three strikes and he's out."

"Don't do that," her friend implored her. "Don't dismiss your feelings just because they're inconvenient. Love is worth fighting for."

"It's not love," Michelle denied emphatically. "I have more self-respect than to put myself second to a man's job again."

"Michelle, most relationships require compromise of some type. It's okay if you don't love him, but don't let childhood grievances keep you from finding true happiness."

"He's testing out a prospective nanny today." Michelle forced cheer into her voice. "Soon he won't need me and I'll be in Los Angeles glad that a fun time didn't keep me from pursuing my dreams."

"Or you could show a little backbone, fight for what you want and start a family with your sweetheart. And his little boy."

"Oh, you think you're funny." Michelle

shook her finger at Amanda. "You are so not funny."

"I'm a little funny." Amanda grinned as she reached for her purse. "Coffee is my treat."

Michelle argued for the bill, but inside she thought Amanda wasn't funny, and the picture she painted held way too much appeal.

"How did you know it was Nate's birthday?" Kim demanded. "I've tried to pry the information from him for three years."

"He left his wallet on the sink, so I checked out his driver's license."

"You looked in his wallet?" Kim sounded awestruck over the phone line.

"Of course. There's a lot to learn about a man in his wallet. Just like a woman's purse. For instance, he's an organ donor, but no surprise there."

"Still it's pretty bold snooping behind his back."

"Oh, he was in the room."

Kim laughed. "That's bolder still."

"So I've reserved the event room at the bowling alley for Friday night. It has the four lanes right in the room. I need you to handle the invitations."

"Sure, I can do that. This is a great idea. A lot of people will be excited to attend."

Michelle believed it. People responded to Nate's strength of character and decency. But who knew she'd find those characteristics so appealing?

"Remember, it's a surprise."

"Got it. How are you going to get him there?"

"It's covered. Hank is going to call and report a fight about a half hour before Nate's shift ends. He's going to specifically ask for Nate to come out."

"That should work. This is a fine thing you're doing, Michelle. You've been good for him."

Michelle had no response to that. They'd certainly been good together, but a lack of any future scared him off. Actually the thought of a future would probably freak him out just as much. The good Lord knew it terrified her.

"He'll probably hate it. He's not one for drawing attention to himself. But he needs a little fuss made over him. I don't think he's had much of that in his life."

"Like I said, you're good for him."

CHAPTER TWELVE

NATE heard from his attorney around two on Friday afternoon. The courts had granted him full custody of Jack.

Raw emotion gripped Nate. He straight-up loved the boy. The depth of it shocked him.

When Jack first arrived Nate hadn't hesitated to accept responsibility for the child. Duty was as familiar to him as brushing his teeth, starting when he was six years old, and it fell to him to care for his mother.

Hell, he'd made a career of it.

With Jack it had become so much more than obligation.

Which was what made him reach into his bottom drawer and pull out the file on Alicia Carlton, Jack's mother. Nate had received notice of her whereabouts shortly after his first meeting with the attorney. Michelle's fervent wish for a mother's love and guidance was the only reason he hadn't pursued legal action against the woman.

She lived in Carson City, Nevada, not much more than an hour away, but clearly out of his jurisdiction.

Thirty-five and divorced, she had a lengthy file. Mostly petty stuff, drug-related, but she spent a year in a secured facility five years ago for being in possession of stolen property.

No doubt about it Jack was better off without her in his life. Yet even with that thought ringing in his head, he closed the file and headed for the door.

He stopped at the dispatcher's desk. "I'm taking a couple of hours of personal time. I'll have my cell on. Hit me if you need me."

She nodded and Nate gave his second in command the same message on his way to his vehicle. An hour and twenty minutes later he pulled into the parking lot of a national restaurant chain and walked inside. He grabbed a seat at the counter and ordered a coffee while he assessed the situation.

One thing he couldn't get out of his head was the timing. Today was his birthday and his cousin Jack had always made a point of talking to him on his birthday. How odd the decision regarding Jack Jr. should be on today of all days. It was almost like Jack Sr. was giving a nod of approval. Nate didn't put a lot of stock in woo-woo stuff. But this felt right.

It took him a few minutes to spot Alicia.

He hardly recognized her. When he last saw her, she'd been four months pregnant, strung out, with sallow skin and her black hair a shaggy, matted mess. She'd barely acknowledged him as he spoke to Jack. His cousin had insisted she was clean, that it was the pregnancy that made her tired. Seemed she suffered from morning sickness.

She looked good today. Her hair was clean and pulled back in a ponytail. Her skin had a healthy sheen and she smiled as she worked.

For the first time Nate saw what had attracted Jack to the woman. She sure didn't appear to be missing her son.

She must have felt the weight of his stare because she glanced up and spotted him. And there it all was for him to see. Fear first, followed by despair, and then hope, and finally resignation.

A lot of emotion in a flash of time, but she didn't try to bolt. She waved him over to a booth by the window before telling her boss she was taking a break.

"How is he?" she demanded as soon as she sat across from him.

Okay, she got points for going there first.

"You left him on the porch in the middle of a snow storm. I could be here to tell you he's dead."

She went white, all the healthy color leaving her face in a rush. "No." She shook her head in denial. "I'd know if he were gone. Somehow, I'd know."

"How could you know? You didn't even wait for me to open the door."

"No, but I saw you. I watched you go in. I couldn't stay, couldn't face you. I was at the lowest point in my life, but I knocked. And I left him in a better place."

"He could have died."

"Could have." She grabbed on to that. "So he's okay?"

"He's fine. Healthy. My attorney just notified me the courts have granted me full custody." He gave it to her straight, no sugar coating.

She went totally still, and then she nodded and her whole body relaxed as she dropped

her head into her hands on the table. No
sound reached him, but by the way her shoulders shook, it appeared she was sobbing her
heart out.

Her boss started toward the table. Nate
flashed his badge and shook his head. The
man backed off, but only as far as the cash
register, where he kept an eye on the booth.

"Ms. Carlton," Nate said after a moment,
and when she didn't respond he said, "Alicia."

One hand broke loose to grab a napkin,
there were motions of mopping up, and then
she slowly lifted her head.

"I'm okay," she told him and straightened
her shoulders. She met his gaze with water-
drenched brown eyes. "It was the right thing
to do."

"You haven't changed your mind?" he
asked her point-blank. If she was having
doubts, he wanted to know now.

"No." Her body shuddered with a heavy
sigh. "I said I reached my lowest point before
I dropped him off at your place. I was wrong.
Losing him was my lowest point. I went on
a real bender after that. I was free, right? No
baby to hold me back or to force me to work
to take care of him."

She dabbed her eyes with the damp napkin. "But no matter what I did, or what I took or drank, I'd see his sweet face in my head. And I'd look at where I was or who I was with and I knew I'd done the right thing in giving him to you. I knew you'd keep him fed and warm and safe. Jack had such faith in you, I knew I could trust you, too."

"You look clean," he stated bluntly. Drugs were not something to tiptoe around.

"I am," she said with her chin up. "For over a month now. I'm doing the best I ever have before. Because of Jack. I was hoping if I stayed clean for a year, you might let me come see him."

He stared at her, searching for a break in her sincerity. He found none.

"But you don't want him back."

Her lips pressed together until they disappeared as if she had to force the words back, but she firmly shook her head. Tears welled again, but she pushed them back.

"I want what's best for him. And that ain't me. A month clean seems like forever. And I got to work at it every day. Real hard. It's best if you keep him." She nodded emphatically and dabbed at the corner of her eye, smiling sadly. "I thought he was a drag on me, but truth is I would be the drag on him. If you want to adopt him, I'll sign whatever you need."

"I'll have my attorney put the papers together." Nate climbed to his feet and put a twenty down for his coffee. "I'll be watching you," he told her, keeping his tone stern. She needed to know he meant what he said. "If you're clean for a year, we'll talk, see if you feel the same way. If you aren't clean, you won't get anywhere near him."

She swallowed hard, then nodded.

He turned away, took a couple of steps and then stopped. He reached into his pocket and pulled out his wallet again. This time he placed a picture Michelle had taken of Jack on the table.

The twenty still sat there and she reached right over it to snap up the picture. Tears flowed down her cheeks. "Thank you."

"Get ready," Kim squealed in excitement. "Hank just called to say a sheriff's car pulled into the lot."

Excited murmurs went around the room as

people jockeyed for a good position to view Nate's surprise.

Michelle stared down at the text on her phone and knew it wasn't Nate driving up. He was going to be late. He'd been to Carson City and was still twenty minutes away. He had something to tell her, but he'd just gotten tagged for a call. He hoped it would be cleared before he got to town. He wanted her to put on something pretty and get Jack ready; they were going out to celebrate tonight.

Her first gut-wrenching reaction was disappointment. The same angry letdown she always experienced when her dad failed to show as expected for some special event.

Well, she knew just how to speed Nate along. Knowing he'd been called to a fight at Hank's Bowl, she texted back: Take your time, Jack and I are at a birthday party at the bowling alley. See you soon.

Her phone immediately rang. Before answering, she walked up next to the bowling lanes where the noise was the loudest. "Hey. I got your text."

"Michelle, are you okay?"

"What?"

"Are you and Jack okay? There was report of a fight."

"You're fighting traffic? Don't worry. We're fine here. Oh, my goodness. What a ruckus."

"Michelle! Go home."

"What? Home? I can barely hear you. Listen, we won't be much longer. We'll see you at the house. Say bye-bye to Daddy, Jack."

Jack cooed on cue, making Michelle grin.

"Wait," Nate demanded.

"Bye." She clicked shut the phone just as Nate's deputy entered the room and a loud boo went up.

Kim rushed up to the man to find out what was up, but Michelle wandered out to watch the parking lot.

Guilt racked her. But she was tired of the men in her life making her wait. Yes, she knew it was part of the job, but she hadn't chosen the job.

Sometimes family should come first.

It didn't help at all that Nate wasn't family. That she had no claim on him or Jack. Or that Nate knew nothing about the party. It didn't even matter that he was much better at keeping her informed of his whereabouts and schedule than her father ever was.

She'd wanted to give him something special and it was ruined because he was late. Glancing around at the crowd waiting to cheer his arrival, she almost regretted putting the surprise together. Almost.

But no. She reined in her emotions. Nate was not her father and she was no longer twelve years old waiting for him to show up at Princess Camp.

The truth was Nate deserved this moment of joy and recognition. She had the feeling he'd had very few happy birthdays. Very few happy moments really.

She bit her lip. Well, it sounded like he'd gotten some good news today; hopefully it would be enough to put him in the mood for the party.

Okay, maybe it was a little mean to let Nate think they were in danger. But she made sure he knew they were both fine. And now he felt compelled to reach the bowling alley as quickly as possible, which was the point.

Ten minutes later Nate's SUV whipped into the lot. He looked grim as he made his way to the building.

Michelle bit her lip and backed into the event room. She hoped she hadn't spoiled his birthday by putting him in a bad mood with her call.

"He's here," she announced to the room.

"Are you sure?" Kim asked after the false alarm earlier.

"Yeah. I saw him."

The blonde clapped her hands. "Goody." She wrapped her arm around David's and dragged him over to crowd close to Michelle near the entrance. "My mother-in-law will probably only stay a short while. She's going to keep Christy overnight and she said she'd be happy to take Jack, too, so you and Nate can enjoy yourselves."

"That would be great." Michelle rubbed Jack's back, disconcerted at the thought of an evening without him. He'd become such a part of her life. "We'll see what Nate says."

A moment later he came charging into the room.

"Surprise!" voices shouted out from all around them.

Nate stopped as if he'd run into a brick wall. He surveyed all the people surrounding him, clearly surprised. Finally he grinned and reached out to shake hands. His gray gazed snagged hers with a promise of retribution before he disappeared in the crush of people.

She sighed and kissed Jack's cheek. "It's going to be all right."

Good. Let him wallow in the attention of his community for a while. He cared for these people whether he knew them as individuals or not. It was time he saw they recognized his dedication.

Yep, let them mellow him out a bit before he hunted her down.

Just as she relaxed with that notion, he appeared in front of her. His eyes flared with heated intent.

"You'll pay for this," he promised as he took Jack, holding the alert baby against his solid shoulder.

She thought that might be it for now. But no, he snaked a hard arm around her waist and jerked her close.

"And never scare me like that again." His head lowered and he kissed her, a slow deep claiming of her mouth by his. Not so much a caress as another promise.

Oh, yeah, if this was her punishment, give

her more. She angled her head and challenged him to do his worst. Best? Hmm. Whatever.

A slap in the face, literally, brought her out of the sensual interlude.

She and Nate both pulled back to find Jack giggling and bouncing. Every day he gained better use of his limbs and he reached out and clocked her again.

"Whoa, kid." Nate caught Jack's arm. "We don't hit women in this family."

"He's just trying to show his love." Michelle grabbed the baby's fist and pretended to take a bite.

"Well, he's going to have to find a different way," Nate stated, pleasant but firm. "Because starting now, no hitting girls."

"You're right," she agreed, rubbing at the smudge of lipstick on his lower lip rather than look into his eyes. He was going to make such a good father and every day her departure loomed closer. "Good job, Daddy."

"Eeek." Jack squealed and waved his arms.

"Are you jealous?" Michelle demanded. "That's it, isn't it?" she teased the baby. "You want all my kisses for yourself."

Jack proved her right by leaning forward to give her a sloppy kiss on the mouth.

"Um." She laughed as she blotted her lips with the back of her hand. "I guess that says it all."

"Now I'm the jealous one," Nate complained.

"Don't worry." She leaned close to whisper. "I'm sure you'll get better with practice."

He caught her chin to hold her near for a lingering kiss where their only connection was mouth to mouth. Slowly, softly, he showed her he knew exactly how to excite her senses. When he lifted his head, she sighed.

"We'll practice more later."

Oh, my. Promises, promises. She didn't know whether to be thrilled or scared. She did know she should discourage him, but she couldn't quite bring herself to do so.

"Nate," a voice called out from the bowling lanes. "We need a man to complete our team."

"Go bowl," she ordered him. "There'll be dancing and karaoke later. It's your party. Have a good time."

"I intend to." He winked and turned to join the bowlers.

While he bowled she kept busy checking on the food and the music. With everything flowing nicely, she slipped out to the car to retrieve the jeans and black polo shirt she'd brought for Nate to change into.

While she was outside, she called the sheriff's office and asked the dispatcher to invite everyone to stop by when they had a chance. The woman was excited to hear from Michelle and assured her everyone would be contacted, both on and off duty because everyone would want to attend or at least stop by.

Tears welled in Michelle's eyes at the show of enthusiasm from Nate's coworkers. He thought he was so alone. But the truth was he collected people and didn't even know it.

Blinking back emotion, she told herself he hadn't worked his magic on her. She may not be running away from River Run anymore. Finding explanations for her father's behavior and seeing his actions through the eyes of an adult had helped her put the ghosts of her childhood behind her. But she was still determined to get to Los Angeles. That's where her future lay.

Back inside she handed off Nate's change of clothes and made a swing around the room, checking that all was well. She got caught up in the noise and gaiety of the party revelers,

grabbed a beer, and strolled over to watch
Nate bowl and let her momentary melancholy
melt away.

CHAPTER THIRTEEN

NATE reluctantly let Jack go home with Kim's mother-in-law. Nate's plan earlier had been to spend the night with Jack and Michelle and it was hard to give that up. But the party was in full swing and she'd gone to a lot of trouble to give him this surprise. So he did his best to get out and mingle.

This was so not his thing. If not for Michelle, he would have been lost. As it was, he kept her in sight. Watching her having fun allowed him to relax and enjoy himself, too.

He killed it at bowling, beating both David and his dad. Okay, so maybe David wasn't so bad. And now Kim belted out a decent rendition of "Redneck Woman." Michelle rocked to the chorus, her hips swaying in sexy rhythm to the beat.

She wore a red minidress, the luxurious material shimmering when she moved. It was a turtleneck halter dress, blousy on the top and snug around her hips. Sheer vixen from head to toe.

He stepped up behind her and wrapped his arms around her waist, pulling her close and swaying along with her. She shimmied against him and then turned in the circle of his arms to face him.

"There's the birthday boy." She linked her arms around his neck. "Having fun?"

"I am."

She laughed. "No need to sound so surprised."

"I'm not a social guy," he said with a shrug.

"That was before you took on the community," she corrected him. "Now they've adopted you."

"Because of you." He had no illusions about that.

"Oh, no." The emphatic shake of her head echoed her denial. "It's all you. I just gave them a venue." She ran her hands over his shoulders, straightened his collar. "What did you want to tell me?"

He made a quick scan of the crowd filling the space. This wasn't the time or the place he'd planned, but good news was good news wherever they were.

"I heard from my attorney today. Jack is officially mine."

Her eyes lit up and she threw her body against him, hugging him tightly. "That is good news. He's so lucky to have you."

Her encouragement eased some of Nate's anxiety. "I'm glad you think so."

"I know so. I've watched the two of you together for the past six weeks. He loves you."

"This is different. The last six weeks felt temporary. This is the rest of our lives. And it is different, stronger. It's as if a link binds us now."

"That makes sense. It's official now."

"Yeah." The tightness in his gut eased even more. "That sounds right. My feelings are the same. I love Jack either way, but now I know no one can take him from me." He told her about his trip over to Carson City and his talk with Jack's mother. "She offered to let me adopt him."

"Really? She said she wanted you to keep him?"

"Yes."

Michelle nodded. "See, even she sees it."

"You were right, that she needs to be a part of his life. If she stays clean, I think they'll be good for each other. If not, then I'll protect him any way I can."

"I have no doubt."

"Okay, everyone," Kim announced from the stage. "We're going to take a break from the karaoke entertainment so someone can give Nate a very special birthday present. Everyone, Michelle Ross."

Applause broke out. And Michelle wiggled out of his grasp.

"That's me." She stepped away, her gaze locked on his. "I hope you like it."

Nate followed her, stopping short of the stage. He crossed his arms over his chest and watched as she picked up a guitar and moved to the stool Kim had set in the middle of the raised dais.

Michelle adjusted the microphone, strummed an introductory riff and began to sing.

My American man wears a uniform,
Does his duty with honor and pride
He suffers every loss both friend and foe
My American man is an everyday hero.

She had the voice of an angel, low and rich, it grabbed him by the heart and squeezed.

My American man wears a badge and a gun.
Protects every man, woman, daughter and son.
His life he'd give and never say no.
My American man is an everyday hero.

My American man opens his arms, opens his home
To a fatherless child, lost and alone.
He heats up the bottle, rocks him to and fro.
My American man is an everyday hero.

My American man takes care of me just right.
He loves me passionately all through the night.
His kisses so sweet, his touch, oh, oh!
My American man is my everyday hero.

The words ended and the music faded away. Silence reigned for a beat of time, and then another before applause broke out, thundering through the room.

Without a word, Nate stepped up to the stage, took Michelle's hand and assisted her down.

"Did you like it?" Her eyes held both excitement and anxiety as she joined him.

Too choked up for words, he kissed her hand and drew her with him across the room.

As he got close to the door, he cleared his throat and called out a deputy's name. When he answered, Nate tossed the man the keys to his SUV. "Drop my vehicle off at my place on your way home."

Nate received a nod. Satisfied, he told Michelle, "Get your purse."

She shook her head. "I locked it in my car."

"Good. Give me the keys." He took them, and laced his fingers through hers. He waved to the crowd and then gave her hand a tug. "Let's go."

He talked little on the trip home, because he didn't know what to say.

She finally broke under the silence. "Are you really mad about the party?"

"No."

"Good." More silence followed. "Then why are you so quiet?"

"Nobody's ever gone to so much trouble for my birthday. Hell, nobody's ever gone to any trouble at all. Mom only remembered events where she got gifts. I got a token present or two at Christmas, but most of the gifts were from her to her. I had to remind her of my birthday." After he turned eight he gave up.

"Did it get any better when you moved in with your uncle?"

"Uncle Stan was simple—birthday, holiday, whatever—he'd pack Jack and me into the car and take us out to dinner. It marked the occasion and that was enough for him."

"My dad and your uncle Stan would have got along real well. That's what he always wanted to do. No surprise I always wanted a party."

"My money is on you."

"And you'd win."

Tonight he couldn't quite grasp it was all for him. Not until Michelle's birthday present. From the moment she stepped onstage, he'd wanted to be alone with her. She looked so pretty in the spotlight. Her silky blond hair flowing like liquid gold around bare white shoulders, lips as red as the dress inching up her long legs. Making him sound like a hero in a voice meant for the bedroom.

It was a gift he'd never forget.

Come to think of it, he'd received a few cards tonight, but thank God nobody else brought gifts. How uncomfortable would that be?

Only when he heard his voice fade did he realize he'd spoken his thought aloud.

"We put it on the invitation not to bring a gift," Michelle explained. "If someone wanted to give something they were encouraged to donate to the River Run Community Improvement Fund."

"I'm not sure you can do that."

"Sure we could. Nobody had to donate. But plenty did. Last I heard you raised twelve hundred dollars for the fund."

"Seriously?" He flashed a glance her way, watched her smother a yawn.

"Yeah." She grinned, her white teeth showing in the spill of a streetlight. "Pretty smart, huh? I knew you wouldn't want people giving you anything, but they're preprogrammed to give for birthdays, so I came up with the donation. The Community Improvement Fund seemed like a good choice, because everyone benefits."

"Brilliant. Are you going to spend the night with me?"

"Is that what you want?"

"More than anything."

"Even if it's not for the best?"

He pulled into the drive, put the car in Park and flipped off the ignition. He turned to her, reached out and cupped the back of her neck, the move instinctive, primal.

"You're leaving. I get that. I want the time we have left to be special."

"It's not the smart thing to do," she reminded him softly.

He drew her close until they were forehead to forehead. "I don't care." He angled his head, placed his lips on hers and gently, oh, so gently, kissed her.

She hesitated, but his care paid off. With a sigh she sank into the caress. Yes, this was what he needed, her in his arms. The taste of her, the warmth of her, his for the taking.

Minutes later he had her upstairs, slowly undressing her like the gift she was. He savored her, with his lips, with every stroke of his hands, with his whole body. And she responded beautifully. Embraced him whole-heartedly, even his scars, her acceptance giving him peace even as his body burned for her.

So receptive, so giving, her pleasure brought him pleasure. And he rocked them ever higher, sensation building on sensation, until anticipation splintered into indescribable satisfaction.

Heaven—he rolled them so he wouldn't crush her—must be something like this.

"Thank you," he said around a throat choked with emotion, "for everything."

Her hand trailed over his chest. "So you liked your song?"

"It's beautiful." He cleared his throat. "More than I deserve."

"Don't say that." She lifted onto her elbow next to him. "You are one of the best men I've ever met."

"There's nothing special about me," he denied.

She laid a finger over his lips, shushing him.

"Everything in that song is true. If you see the value of it, you have to see the value in yourself."

He frowned, wanting to argue with her logic but unable to do so.

Seeing she'd stumped him, she smiled and cuddled next to him again. "My agent loved it. She's sending it to an up-and-coming star in Nashville."

"Good luck." He sighed, feeling something deep inside settle. Life had never been better.

Jack was his now, safe and sound. As contentment led him into sleep, Nate tightened his arms around the beauty sleeping bonelessly beside him. Michelle was his, too. For as long as she stayed.

Michelle put the finishing touch to the chair rail in the master bedroom. She stepped back and admired the freshness of the room. As with all the renovations she'd done to the house, her improvements in here were mostly cosmetic, bringing the interior design from mid-eighties to the new millennium.

The chair rail circled the room in a soft cream; above it a mellow green paint three shades lighter than the sage green below the rail gave the room a serene feel. Cream curtains held back with sage ties dressed the window. A luxurious light green comforter with dark green vines flowing over it and mounds of pillows propped at the head made the bed an inviting bower. An artful rug in reverse colors and pattern from the comforter brought life to the serviceable beige carpet.

Pleased with the room she did a little happy dance. It hit the perfect balance, pretty without being too feminine. The dark wood of the furniture added the right masculine touch.

Satisfied, she headed in to check on the progress of the electrician in the master bath. She'd bought new light fixtures for the whole house. The electrician started the day inspecting the wiring throughout, and Michelle was happy to hear everything was in good shape. Now he was wrapping up the installation of the new fixtures.

Her cell rang before she reached the bathroom. She saw her agent's name and anticipation tingled up her spine.

"Hi, Denise. Tell me quick so I can breathe, do you have news about the song?"

"Girl, would I mess with you? Would I chatter on about nothing while you waited breathlessly for me to give you exciting news? It's not like you haven't been waiting for this news forever—"

"Denise, tell me now or I swear to you I will come through this line and scuff up your Jimmy Choos."

A husky laugh sounded. "Is that any way to talk to the woman who is going to make all your dreams come true?"

"Oh, my God." Michelle's heart stuttered. "She wants to buy the song?"

"She wants to buy the song."

Michelle screamed. Too excited to contain it she danced for real and when the electrician came running to see what happened, she grabbed him and danced some more.

"Ah, congratulations." Balding and in his fifties, the man gave her a twirl and a hug and then wiggled free and escaped back to the bathroom.

Michelle laughed and finally heard Denise calling her name. She put the cell back to her ear. "Sorry about that, I got a little carried away."

"You're entitled." Denise sounded almost as excited as Michelle felt. "It's a great song. I heard a man's voice, the inspiration for your song perhaps?"

"Electrician. Poor man now knows how it feels to be groped."

"It's his lucky day. And yours, too. I hope you're done with that house, because it's time to move to L.A."

"She's really, seriously interested in the song? Don't mess with me about this, Denise."

"Michelle, this is serious business. I would never mess with you over the sale of your song."

"I need to sit down." Michelle sank right down to the green rug.

"She loved the song. Wants to make it a lead on her next album."

"Shut up." This was so surreal. "Are you going to tell me who she is?"

"Rikki West, she won *Idol* a couple of years ago. Has been riding a wave to the top ever since."

"I can't believe it." Michelle couldn't be more thrilled. She loved Rikki West's voice. "I thought of her when I was writing it. This is perfect."

"It gets better." Denise practically purred. "She wants to meet you, to see what else you have."

"When? Where?" Okay, this had to be a dream. Michelle pinched herself because it was just too good to be true. The sting on her left arm did little to convince her she wasn't in some alternate reality.

"She's going to be in L.A. for an awards show next week. You need to get yourself down here now."

"Right." Michelle frowned, there was no reason the request should throw her. She'd always known the time would come for her to leave.

The first time Denise mentioned it Michelle had been too swept up in the moment to make the connection that going to L.A. meant leaving River Run. And Jack.

It meant the end of what she had with Nate.

Denise gave Michelle a few more details and signed off with another nudge to finish her business in River Run and get her butt to Los Angeles.

Her stomach churned and she flopped back on the carpet to stare up at the ceiling and try and make sense of what she was feeling.

Oh, God. She didn't want to go.

The biggest break of her career and her heart broke at the idea of leaving River Run and the family she'd found here.

No, she just felt attached because she was

missing her dad, that's all. She'd reassigned her affections to keep from being so lonely. And sure she'd miss Nate and the baby for a few days. But her new life would soon distract her.

And she'd see them again. She still had to come back and sell the house. So no more moping. Today was going to be all about celebrating.

Needing her buzz back, she called Amanda in San Francisco and linked in Elle in San Diego. Both screamed when they heard her news.

"I knew it would happen." Elle calmed first. "You're so talented it was only a matter of time."

"And it's a great song," Amanda added. "I heard it when she came to town to record it. Patriotic is always in and it ends kind of like a love song, which is a nice touch. Makes me wonder if there's anything you want to tell us?"

No, not a thing. Michelle wasn't going down that road again.

"I can tell you Denise wants me in Los Angeles yesterday."

"Let me know when you make your reservations," Elle told her. "I'll drive up and help you find a place to live. We can celebrate."

"Count me in," Amanda demanded. "I'll take the weekend off from the museum and fly down, too. Heck, I'll bring the champagne."

CHAPTER FOURTEEN

"Hey, I got your message and yes, I'll be home at the regular time. See you tonight."

After leaving Michelle the voice mail, Nate flipped his cell closed and returned it to his pocket. She wanted to tell him something at dinner. He had a bad feeling he knew what it was.

She was leaving.

And he wasn't ready to hear it.

A glance at his watch told him he had two hours before end of shift. He bent his head down and put his attention into completing the budget report for the mayor. But Nate's mind soon wandered.

The two weeks since his birthday had shown him what it meant to be part of a loving family. Waking up to Michelle each morning, watching Jack learn something new every day, knowing she had his back at home—Nate never expected to know such joy.

After half an hour, he acknowledged the report was a no-go. He couldn't concentrate, couldn't stand to sit still. Pushing to his feet, he left his office. He needed to be busy. Stay busy.

He stopped at dispatch. "What do we have going on?"

"It's quiet," she told him. "But I just got a call from Frank over at the Sleepy Bear Motel. He says someone broke into all his units and stole the complimentary toiletries. I was going to send Nelson."

"I'll take it." A nuisance call was a perfect time-suck. And it would keep him distracted for the rest of his shift. "Have Nelson come in if it looks like Peters needs help."

Michelle sounded excited on the phone. He knew she'd scheduled the electrician to come today. She'd come to refurbish and sell the house. The electrician marked the end of that project. There was nothing more to hold her in town until his lease ended in two months.

The thought of her leaving tore him apart. He could deny it no longer. He loved her. He didn't know what he was going to do when she left town. He'd finally found the peace he sought in the arms of a siren. Michelle was not the shallow woman he'd first thought. Beautiful and strong, clever and funny, she was a survivor, like him. And he'd fallen in love.

Ten minutes later he arrived at the Sleepy Bear Motel to find the owner—Frank—nose to nose with Beverly, the owner of the local B and B. Uh-oh. Everyone knew of the ongoing feud between the gangly, gray-haired Frank and the plump, grandmotherly redhead.

This might take a little longer than he thought.

"Okay, let's break it up here." Nate quickly put himself between the two of them before the heated argument got out of control.

"Frank accused my grandson of stealing the toiletries." Beverly tried to get around Nate. "No one is going to call my grandson a thief."

It took him a few minutes to calm them down and separate them so he could conduct interviews. And then he had to find a spot to speak to one while keeping an eye on the other.

Just when he was wrapping up the statements, pleased to be only ten minutes past his end of shift, Frank's granddaughter showed up. She went ballistic when she heard Frank had accused the grandson.

"Grandpa, I told you he's smart. He doesn't have to steal. I love him."

Nate smothered a groan. He was tempted to order the lot of them down to the station, but that would only drag this out and he was already late. He reached for his phone to call Michelle and the grandson stormed in and, like his grandmother, immediately went nose to nose with Frank.

Nate pushed his phone into his pocket and went to break it up.

Tears blurring her vision, Michelle blew out the candles on the dining room table. In the kitchen she ditched the chicken medallions in artichoke sauce, pan and all, into the trash. Followed by the bread, the salad and the baked potatoes.

Ruined. Everything was ruined.

The food, the dinner, the joy in sharing her news with Nate, all of it ruined because of his tardiness, because he couldn't be bothered to call and tell her he was going to be late.

Bad enough to be late, but at least call, then she knew better than to expect him at any minute, knew to do something with the food before it grew cold, dry and wilted. Then she knew that her excitement had no foundation, that she was second to the job, again.

She scrubbed the tears from her face, furious at their appearance. She would not cry today.

It was the best day of her life.

She'd be damned if she'd cry.

She'd be damned if she'd stay in this hick town one more night.

She was right to leave River Run when she was younger, right that there was nothing here for her. Tonight proved that.

Her phone rang. She looked at the caller ID. Nate. Looked at the time, over an hour late. She rejected the call.

Chin up, shoulders back, she raced upstairs. In her room she threw her suitcases on the bed and began piling in clothes. She tried for order but folding was beyond her.

She shook with anger, with disappointment.

The betrayal was her own. He wasn't supposed to matter. Men were for fun and a means to an end. She knew that, had learned early to rely only on herself.

Because it hurt when she trusted someone with her heart and they let her down. And they always let her down. Second to the job again. It was the one thing she promised herself in a relationship. She must come first.

The disillusionment was all her fault. He was a lawman, so of course giving her priority was the one thing he couldn't promise her. And yeah, she'd been lying to herself every time she pretended she could walk away without looking back.

All the more reason to be gone when he got home. No need to put her pain on display. He didn't deserve her tears, didn't deserve her love.

Suddenly weak, she sank down on the side of the bed. Oh, God. She loved him.

Oh, yeah, she was a monster liar. How could she let this happen? She knew better than to leave her heart vulnerable. But he'd stolen past her guard with his broken soul and ready acceptance of Jack.

Jack. Oh, Lord.

Her throat tightened and she surged to her feet, seeking action to offset the need to think, to stop the emotions bombarding her from all sides.

The closet and drawers were empty so her gaze went to the walls, the bed. She hadn't touched this room mostly because she didn't want the mess in here where she slept but also because the nostalgia of it, in the face of her father's loss, made her feel safe, loved.

Another illusion.

Armed with anger and righteousness she stripped the walls of posters and pictures, of butterflies and musical notes. Books and trinkets got tossed into a box as she removed all evidence of herself from the room.

That done she carried her bags downstairs.

And there her emotion-driven adrenaline rush gave out on her. She looked at the door and couldn't bring herself to walk through it.

Her phone rang again. Nate again. She rejected it again.

As much as she hurt, the truth was Nate and Jack had her heart. She couldn't just leave. Instead she turned and headed out back, going where she always went as a child when she didn't know what to do and she needed to think.

She escaped to her castle.

* * *

By the time Nate got everything sorted out—all signs pointed to the new maid, who had missed her shift and was nowhere to be found—and got on the road home, he was nearly two hours late.

He tried Michelle's cell again. He'd finally managed a try twenty minutes ago but it went to voice mail. And it was the same now.

Aggravated, he tossed the phone into the passenger seat. Her refusal to answer was not good. Told him just how much trouble he faced.

He wasn't eager to hear her departure was imminent, yet he didn't want to hurt her, either. And this whole episode smacked of her father's neglect. Nate usually managed to connect with her to let her know he'd be late, but today's situation had been too volatile. Petty, yes, but emotions had been running hot.

He nearly tripped over her bags when he walked through the door. It reminded him of the day she arrived, of finding her asleep on his couch. Of the kiss that brought him to life. From that moment on, he hadn't been able to get her out of his head.

"Michelle," he called out and dread weighed heavy on him when silence answered him.

The very notion of losing her tore his soul in half. Yes, he had to let her go, but not like this, not on bad terms.

His nose led him to the kitchen. The savory scent of dinner lingered in the air and he found the remains of it in the trash. He rescued the pan, considered it another bad sign and continued his search for her.

Her room broke his heart. Seeing her childhood memories torn from the walls and stuffed in the trash shredded something deep inside him. It also told him he may be wrong about what she wanted to tell him. This was not careful packing. This was rage fueled by hurt.

More than ever he regretted taking the nuisance call. Not that he could know it would turn into such a fiasco, except a cop always knew a call could turn into something more.

He needed to find her. Needed to make this better. He backed into the hall and stared into Jack's empty room. It struck him, where was the baby?

He flipped open his phone, called Kim.

"Yeah, I have Jack. Michelle asked me to

take him for the night. Are you sure she's not there? She was headed home to make dinner when she left here."

"The dinner is here." What was left of it. "She's not."

"She was excited about something but said she'd tell me about it tomorrow. She wanted to tell you first."

"I was a little late."

"Uh-oh."

"Yeah. Hey, thanks for watching Jack."

"Good luck."

He went back, checked every room looking for Michelle. She was nowhere yet everywhere. She'd taken a house stuck in the eighties and turned it into a modern, comfortable home. With paint and molding, new rugs and fixtures and a lot of hard work she'd changed it from sorry and dated to fresh and inviting.

He'd thought about buying the house from her, but no. He couldn't live here without her.

The quiet ate at him. He used to live in silence. There had been times when lack of noise meant the difference between survival or death. But that wasn't who he was anymore.

He was a dad now. Noise came with the territory.

He hadn't made a big deal of it when Michelle, talking to Jack, had first referred to him as Daddy, but the name felt good. He probably wouldn't have claimed the title without her, would just have gone on as Uncle Nate. But he wanted to be a dad, wanted the bond and responsibility implied by the title. Wanted to give Jack the love and connection he deserved.

And still it wouldn't be enough for Nate. Michelle completed their little family. These last couple of weeks of playing make-believe family showed him just what he'd be missing.

Sure he could hire someone to do the things she did but it wouldn't be the same. She challenged him, encouraged him, made him laugh. She sang like an angel and made love like a vixen. She wanted to be catered to yet worked like a dog when it mattered to her. He'd miss how she enjoyed cooking but got lazy over the laundry.

Most of all he'd miss her smile and the look in her eyes when she said his name.

The look in her eyes. The look that said she thought the world revolved around him.

How could she look at him like that and not love him?

Ha. He laughed out loud. She loved him.

Hope energized him. If she loved him, he had a chance. Spurred to new action he moved from the hall to the kitchen.

He puzzled over whether the wreck in her bedroom happened before the trashing of the dinner when a light in the tree house caught his attention. Of course.

"Michelle," he called as he stepped outside. No response. Not surprised he powered his way up the ladder and shouldered through the child-size door.

Wrapped in a soft pink throw she slept with her head on a purple pillow shaped like a crown. The light behind her made her hair glow like ribbons of flowing gold. Again he remembered the day she first arrived.

Unhesitating he claimed his sleeping beauty with a kiss. He ran his tongue along the seam of her mouth and nibbled lightly on her bottom lip. Soon she blossomed under his attention, her passion awakening with her senses.

Michelle came awake to a warm embrace and the familiar taste of Nate. His kiss took her from slumberous to aroused from one racing heartbeat to the next. She longed to wrap her arms around his neck and hold on tight.

Instead she sighed and pushed against his chest. "I'm mad at you."

"Yeah, I got that from the pan in the trash."

"I worked hard on that dinner."

"I'm sorry I missed it. Sorry I upset you."

She narrowed her eyes at him. "You can do better than that."

"You're right." He swept a curl back from her face, his gaze following the gesture. And then his glance met hers and the intensity in his gray eyes made her breath catch. "I love you."

"Oh, no." Her heart rejoiced even as she denied his words. "Don't say that." Unable to hold his gaze she looked away. "Don't make this harder."

"I am going to make it hard." He kissed her cheek, the line of her jaw. "I'm going to fight for you."

"We're totally wrong for each other," she reminded him. "You love this town and I've been waiting to leave since the moment I got here."

"We belong together." He nudged her nose

with his, then dipped down to kiss the corner of her mouth. She turned into the caress, instinctively seeking more, but he'd already moved on. "And you made your peace with River Run when you made peace with your father's memory."

"You're a cop." Let him argue that one after leaving her sitting for nearly two hours tonight. "I vowed never to be with a cop."

"Too late." He lowered his head to the curve of her neck. "We've been lovers for a month. These last two weeks waking up next to you have been magical."

"No."

"Ah, ah. Your honesty is one of the things I love most about you." The heat of his tongue tasted her skin. "And we're more than lovers, we're a family."

"No." She shook her head. "No fair bringing Jack into this."

"All's fair in love and war." He breathed against her ear, making the cliché a carnal threat. "I'm a warrior in love. I'm going to fight to win."

"Nate."

"He loves you. We love you."

"Unfair, unfair." He was destroying her

with his relentless pursuit combined with a delicious physical attack. How did she fight him when she couldn't think straight?

"I'm leaving."

"Stay. Marry me. Be Jack's mom."

"I sold my song," she whispered desperately as he nibbled on her earlobe. She needed a reminder of where her future was. "The one I wrote about you."

That stopped him. He lifted onto his elbow, ending his sensual assault to stare down at her. His expression revealed nothing but she could practically see his mind at work.

She held her breath. It was her song, but his, too, and he was a very private man.

Finally he nodded and she breathed. And then his face lit up with pride and joy for her. "Congratulations."

And that was the moment he won her over. His approval and excitement for her warmed her heart. She'd been waiting for this minute since she got the call. But everything she'd always wanted was suddenly at odds with what she'd never wanted but had found where she least expected.

"I need to be in Los Angeles next week."

She loved Nate, loved Jack, but how did she give up her dream?

"Michelle…" He cradled her face in his hands, demanded she look him in the eyes. "I was late tonight because a call went long. I hurt you and I'm sorry. I'm not going to lie to you. There are times you'll have to be second to my job, but I'm willing to be second to yours occasionally, too. We'll decide on a nanny so you can write and fly when you need to. As long as I'm first in your heart like you are in mine, we can make it work. Go to L.A. but come home to me."

"I can go to Los Angeles? And Nashville?" First in his heart. She liked the sound of that. Was it possible she could have it all? Love, a family and her career?

"Tell me you love me and I'll drive you to the airport. But you have to promise to marry me first."

She threw her arms around his neck and dragged him down to her, kissing him with everything in her. He wrapped her close and delivered on his erotic onslaught.

"Yes," she accepted, feeling lucky as the princess she used to dream of being. "I love you. Yes, I'll marry you. Yes, I'll be Jack's mom. But be warned. You proposed in a castle. I'll settle for nothing less than happily ever after."

He grinned. "No problem. I have my very own sleeping beauty." To prove it, he kissed her again.

* * * * *